GREY FEATHERS

A Dystopian Urban Fantasy Novel

Angels of the Apocalypse
Book 2

CINDY CARROLL

Hanlon Creek Press

Grey Feathers
Angels of the Apocalypse Book 2

by Cindy Carroll

ePub ISBN: 978-1-7770055-3-5

Print ISBN: 978-1-7770055-7-3

Edited by Lawrence Editing

All characters in this book are fiction and figments of the author's imagination. www.cindycarroll.com

For my husband, always

Author's Note

While going through edits of this book it became obvious that I would have to go with Canadian spellings. With official names like Toronto Armoury Military Base and Canadian Defence Research and Development, I couldn't spell those any other way. Which led to having to make changes to other words to remain consistent. Grey was always going to have the e. You will also find words with an added u (savour, flavour, etc.), or an added l (swivelling, travelling, etc.) plus that pesky c in defence. Most words with a z in the American version (analyze, generalize, etc.) are acceptable in Canadian spelling with the z (zed) so those remain.

Chapter One

If she shook one more hand, Becky Malak was sure it would fall off. The delicate limb tingled from overuse at Toronto's busiest soup kitchen. Not from doling out meals, but from shaking hands with almost every person who went through the line. And with the TV camera with CTBN emblazoned on the side ever present, and Henry, her cameraman, pointing it at her every second they'd been there, her cheeks ached from smiling. It was only Monday evening, but a week's worth of stress settled on her shoulders.

All that work, and she didn't feel a quiver of angelic magic returning to her wings. She'd come to the soup kitchen, on her own time, to bring awareness to the plight of the homeless in the city. For the hour they'd been there, she'd observed staff, talked to patrons, gotten to know some of the most vulnerable in the city. Yet no reward.

When the red light above the camera blinked out, she sighed. "That's a wrap."

Henry grabbed his gear. "You need a ride?"

"No, I'm meeting my sisters for drinks. I can walk."

They parted at the door to the soup kitchen. He went left toward the next street over where the van was parked, and she went right toward Queen Street West. Her sisters were fellow fallen angels, all of them stuck on Earth, trying to earn back their power so they could stop an apocalypse. Then return home.

Standing at the traffic lights at Queen Street West and York Street, she shivered as a December breeze ruffled the edges of her coat. If she had more of her angelic power back, the cold wouldn't affect her. A noise to her left kicked her reporter's instincts into high gear. Heart pounding, she followed the sound of an alarm, her heels clacking along the sidewalk as she rushed toward the commotion.

A crowd gathered in front of a pawnshop about fifty feet away on Queen Street West. A man in his mid-twenties raced by her, his hand gripping a bag that jangled as he ran. An older man stumbled out of the shop, looked both ways along the sidewalk, then stumbled toward her.

Becky dug her phone out of her purse, swiped to open it, and called her producer.

"Ellen, I'm on scene at what looks like a robbery at a pawnshop. Can you send Henry back? This will tie into my series of stories about increasing crime in the city." She bit her lip at the thought of ruining her cameraman's evening. How annoyed would he be that he had to come back?

The sigh on the other end irked her. "Keep it short. We'll use it as a tie-in."

She agreed, shoved her phone into her back pocket, and watched the older man attempt to run after the robber. Before he could get to the intersection, he slowed, staggered, and fell to the ground. Becky ran over. Blood soaked through the man's shirt.

"We need some help here!" She pulled out her phone again and called 911.

A woman emerged from the pawnshop and let out a gasp when she spotted the man on the ground. She rushed over, tears streaming down her face. Becky's sister Sarah raced forward. Focused on the robbery, she hadn't noticed any of her sisters were close by.

"I'm a doctor. Step away from him, ma'am, so I can take a look. Do you have a first aid kit?" When the woman nodded, Sarah said, "Good. I need you to get it for me."

Becky's sister, Sarah, knelt by the prone man, concerned doctor expression in place. Behind her, Rachel, holding the guy with the bag by the arm, and Leah walked toward the scene. Rachel spoke into her phone and nodded, then tucked it into her jeans pocket.

"Off duty for less than an hour, and who do I stumble across? Tony, so nice to see you again." Rachel sneered as she pulled out handcuffs from her back pocket.

Being robbed by the Grange's enforcer meant the pawnshop owner likely didn't have enough to pay for protection this week. The bag of goods might be forced compensation for that oversight. Despite a raid on the gang's headquarters, the group was still operating with a handful of members who managed to get out on bail.

The woman stood shakily, keeping an eye on the man, no doubt her husband. She looked at Rachel, a tremulous smile barely touching her lips. "Thank you so much for catching him."

"You're welcome, ma'am. I can't take the credit. A helpful bystander tripped him. Fell right at my feet."

Rachel's expression changed for a split second and she did a little shiver. Becky peeked around her, her cloaked wings visible only to angels, and saw a new patch of white forming in the feathers near Rachel's shoulder. Teeth clenched, pain throbbed in Becky's jaw. How was that fair? Becky, after coming from volunteering at a soup kitchen and now calling 911 to save a man's life, received no reward of power.

The woman hurried off to retrieve the first aid kit from the shop.

Becky's cameraman arrived, jogging along the sidewalk, camera clutched at his side like it weighed nothing. His expressionless face caused a knot to form in her stomach. Later, at the TV station, she would promise to make it up to him. In such a short amount of time, what plans could he have had?

While Sarah worked on the man, Becky fluffed her hair and checked her makeup. Another sound bite for her series on increasing crime in the city confirmed things were deteriorating faster than they could fix anything. She snapped her fingers to get Henry's attention.

"Get ready. I want to get a shot of Dr. Malak working on the owner of the shop."

The woman brought the first aid kit. Sarah flipped it open and pulled out gauze and medical tape. Despite the cold air, her hands remained steady as she worked on her patient.

Becky gently pulled the woman aside so Sarah could work. "Ma'am, could you tell me what happened here?"

Tears streamed down the woman's face. She shook in the cold December air. She pointed to the man Rachel expertly held, despite him struggling to escape. "That man came into our shop and shot my husband even after we'd handed over what he wanted."

"Your husband didn't have a weapon to scare him away?"

It sucked asking questions like that, but anything could

set a criminal off, thinking the owner deserved it because they attempted to stop them. Criminals were getting bolder, more violent. It was like they were having fun. It wasn't just robbing to be able to survive. Greed. Plain and simple. No respect for anyone else's belongings. They'd vanquished Conquest, but another horseman had to be here already, influencing the population, nudging them toward chaos.

Becky nodded to her cameraman. When the record light went on, she waited for his countdown.

"This is Becky Malak, live on the scene of a robbery in downtown Toronto. The owner of a pawnshop was brutally shot after handing over goods to a robber."

Becky walked over to Rachel. Her sister frowned but didn't move. "Detective Rachel Malak with the homicide division valiantly caught the suspect. And Dr. Sarah Malak of Queen City Hospital is working on the owner."

Sarah didn't look up, continuing to work on her patient.

Becky schooled her face into a mask of seriousness. "Violence in the city continues to be a problem, bleeding out to encompass all of the Greater Toronto Area and beyond the GTA. When will it stop?"

Sadly, she and her sisters knew the answer to that. It wouldn't stop until they put a halt to the apocalypse already in progress. After slowing down rival gangs and vanquishing Conquest, none of their efforts seemed to have made a dent. Circumstantial evidence abounded that another horseman was already there, working in the background.

Sirens screamed, growing louder as the ambulance got closer.

"This is Becky Malak, reporting from Queen Street West."

The cameraman nodded and the recording light went off. "Do you still need me?"

Becky took a deep breath of the cold night air. His feet pointed away from her, as if he wanted to be anywhere else. She didn't think she was that bad to work with, but it was getting late. He probably had a life he wanted to get back to, a girlfriend who wanted to spend time with him.

"Nothing else. Good job tonight. Thanks. See you tomorrow."

His eyes widened. "Thanks. Good night."

Ignoring his surprise, she turned her attention back to Sarah and the shop owner. The bleeding had stopped, and Sarah was continuing to apply pressure while also checking his vitals as best as she could. He stirred.

"Try to stay still," Sarah said. "An ambulance is on the way."

His wife, fingers white from pressing them against her mouth, nodded, smiled. Tears poured down her cheeks.

The outcome of her sister's ministrations would make a good follow-up in the morning.

A larger crowd of onlookers had gathered. Some curious, some attention seekers trying to get into frame, some neighbours worried about the owner. They parted for the EMTs newly arrived on the scene. Jason, the EMT who had looked after Rachel after she'd been shot in a botched drive by shooting on the Grange's headquarters, rushed forward with his gear, knelt beside the prone man, and smiled a greeting at Sarah.

Sarah rattled off the man's information, approximate age, vitals, severity of the wound. Jason took over.

"Thanks, we've got it from here."

Sarah smiled and turned back to the man's wife. "He's in good hands."

Rachel stepped forward, tipping her head to the side.

"You aren't going with him to the hospital? They're probably taking him to yours."

Sarah shook her head. "I'm off duty, and he couldn't be in better hands with the EMTs and staff at the hospital."

A shiver went through Sarah. Dismayed, Becky peeked at Sarah's cloaked wings. A small spot of white grew two centimetres larger. How was it fair that Rachel got power back for essentially doing her job? And Sarah got power back for not going to the hospital to do hers?

Uniformed constables arrived on scene and Rachel handed over the suspect to them. Properly handcuffed and informed of his arrest, they carefully put him in the backseat of the police cruiser. When Rachel finished talking to them, she darted back over to where Becky stood with Sarah and Leah.

Releasing a long breath, Becky nodded at the departing emergency vehicles. "What a night. Are you guys ready for those drinks now?"

Baron's was close to the crime scene, a short walk from work for all of them except Leah, since she fell from Heaven last, and not far from their loft. It had been the perfect spot to hash out their problems. And with the violence in the city getting worse by the day, they didn't have a lot of time to nip the apocalypse in the bud.

Her phone buzzed and she pulled it out of her pocket. Anytime, night or day, if she wasn't sleeping, she tried to read and respond to whatever came through. She never knew when it would be work, an expert helping with an ongoing story, the public relations person from the police.

This time, it was an informant. Possibly the same one who had tipped her off before about a government secret. This one said something that sent a chill down her spine.

What was really in the flu vaccine this year?

X

Half an hour later, they sat at the back of Baron's, listening to the owner's playlist while the band took a break. Becky tapped her foot up and down to the beat of the music. She took a sip of her beer. The cool amber liquid tickled her throat. Talking for a living meant she needed to take care of her voice, but she still liked to indulge in beer on occasion.

Rachel plunked her empty glass on the table. "How did the bail hearing go for our doppelgänger of Victor?"

Though their bruises from their fight against Conquest had healed, the altercation still lingered in Becky's memory. For a moment, she'd thought they wouldn't be able to send him back and replace him with a poppet who would do no more damage.

"Since he was technically the leader of the Grange gang, the judge set bail pretty high. As far as I know, it hasn't been posted yet, though."

Rachel leaned back in her chair, giving Sarah a pointed look when the doctor swiped a French fry from her plate. Rachel pulled the plate closer to herself.

"Good. Maybe more time in lockup will help some of the other prisoners. Since he's now technically an instrument of angels, maybe some of that will rub off on the others."

Becky nodded distractedly. "Maybe."

She pulled out her phone and read the anonymous text message again. Every year, conspiracy theories abounded about the flu vaccine. There were as many arguments against getting the vaccine as there were for getting it. Because of a news story she'd done a few weeks ago, she knew the number of vaccines administered was higher than in the previous five years. Social media posts about the vaccine making you sick and a myriad other reasons not to have it, were down. But now this.

What was really in the flu vaccine this year?

X

She frowned. How different could it be from year to year?

"You've been looking at that thing since before we left the crime scene." Sarah snatched Becky's phone and hit the home button to activate the screen.

The doctor's eyebrows drew together. "Is this from an anonymous source?"

Becky grabbed the phone back. "It would appear. Do you know what it means? Was there something different in the flu vaccine this year?"

Sarah shrugged. "There was nothing unusual about the listed ingredients. They were the same as they have been every year, with minor modifications for strain, of course."

"You're sure? Nothing jumped out at you this year?"

"I'm sure. I've been giving them out at the hospital's clinic since the end of October. You think there's something bad in them this year based on an anonymous text?"

Becky read the message for the hundredth time, willing some sort of understanding that never came. She wouldn't find out tonight. Maybe a good night's sleep and a fresh perspective in the morning would shed some light on the matter.

"I'll send it to my assistant, see what she can dig up."

Becky took a screenshot of the message and sent it to Laura with a note to look into it for her. Putting it out of her mind for the time being, she placed the phone face down on the table and took a sip of her drink. There was plenty of time to investigate tomorrow. She had a feeling the anonymous source wouldn't let that be the only message if they felt she wasn't doing anything with the information. Was she the only reporter they were messaging? Maybe there were reporters all over the city with the same tip. But only she was a fallen angel. The churning in her gut told her this had to do with the already in progress apocalypse. Maybe it would hold a clue for halting the end of the world.

The scroll of news across the TV above the bar caught Becky's attention. It was the usual stuff about robberies in the city, the murder count for the year closing in on the highest it'd ever been since the province started tracking that statistic. A brief scroll about peace talks that resumed in Prague that morning after a brief hiatus made her stomach tighten. A lump formed, churning her insides. Peace talks sounded good, until you realized it was the last step before war. If the talks failed, countries would attack each other.

She pointed at the TV. The rest of her sisters read the snippet.

"That's not good." Rachel shook her head and ate another fry. "Williams and I are going to be very busy, I suspect."

"If we're at the peace talks stage, it's worse than we thought," Leah said.

When the news had started talking about the peace talks weeks ago, she hadn't thought they'd actually happen. The rest of the world was relatively stable, except for the weather phenomena indicating an apocalypse. But now that the peace talks were underway, it didn't bode well for the rest of the planet.

Becky drummed her fingers on the table. "That means War has to be here already, right? We sent Conquest back, but War was summoned."

Rachel nodded. "By that priest. For all we know, he's the head of the Omega sect doomsday cult."

Becky's phone pinged and she glanced at it as a message from her intern was disappearing from the screen. Laura would look into the flu vaccine and get back to her tomorrow in the office. Not that she expected anything earth-shattering. This might be a wild goose chase or a conspiracy theory with no real evidence.

"Have you noticed anything unusual going on?" She pierced Rachel with a stare.

"Not really. The gangs have settled now that they think Victor is in jail, but that won't last long. Someone will try to take over as leader."

"What about you?" Leah stabbed a grape tomato with her fork. "Anything warlike coming across the news wires?"

Becky shook her head. "Except for the peace talks, of course. There's nothing else that looks odd yet."

Bothered by the anonymous tip, she picked up her phone again and read the message a few more times, hoping that somehow the message would have more information in it this time.

Sarah snagged a tomato from Leah's plate and popped it into her mouth. "What's bothering you about that message? You get anonymous tips all the time."

Becky shrugged. "Not sure. But my reporter sense is tingling."

Later that evening, Becky and Leah stood in front of Darla and her fellow sex workers in the basement of their building. Rachel and Sarah, exhausted from work and a training session to keep them prepared for a fight, relaxed up in the loft. Darla and her friends sat attentively, eager to learn. When they'd decided to teach the sex workers about finances and self-defence, they'd pooled some of their power and magically added classroom-style rooms in the basement. Becky held up a notebook and pen.

"Today, we're going to talk about finance," Becky began. "It's important to understand how money works, so you can take control of your own finances and make the most of what you have."

Leah took over. "First, let's start with budgeting. Write down your monthly income and expenses, and make sure your expenses don't exceed your income. This way, you'll be able to save some money each month."

Darla raised her hand. "What do we do with the money we save?"

Becky smiled. "Good question. You can put it into a savings account, or invest it in a stock or mutual fund. Just make sure to do your research and understand the risks involved."

With Rachel keeping an eye on the sex workers, their pimps weren't as violent or greedy as they used to be. The gangs who oversaw the pimps got by with a little less. At least for now. It wouldn't be long before the Grange decided the sex workers should be paying them more.

Leah continued, "It's also important to have an emergency fund. Set aside some money each month for unexpected expenses, like medical bills or car repairs."

The women took notes and asked questions, soaking up the information. After an hour of discussing finance, Becky and Leah declared the lesson complete.

"Remember, it's important to be prepared for anything," Becky said. "So don't forget about your self-defence training. We'll be here to help you learn how to protect yourself."

Rachel had saved Darla from the Grange's enforcer and now the angels wanted to make sure the sex workers could take care of themselves.

The women nodded, filing out of the room and chatting away about what they'd learned. Becky hated that they were about to go walk the streets in order to make the money they'd be putting away for a rainy day.

A few minutes before midnight, Gunther Fertig sat in his office in the Toronto Armoury Military Base, scrolling through the information Conquest had left him before being vanquished back to limbo. He knew the horseman no longer walked the Earth because he could feel that he was the only whole one here. Death, of course, was always around because his reapers needed to do their job. But Conquest had been bested and now the plan might fall behind. Good thing he didn't need sleep like the mere mortals who took up space on the planet.

Gunther paused in his perusal of the information to read Victor's notes about Caleb Bishop more closely. Close to choosing darkness over light, what caught his attention was Victor's note about the young man's soul. Not many of those around after Death did his work in purgatory, eliminating as many as he could to fast forward the start of the apocalypse.

Victor's notes mentioned the man's troubles at home, the grudging acceptance from the gang, and the man's potential to be a right-hand when the end of the world came. If the right buttons were pushed.

Gunther leaned back in his leather chair, put his hands behind his head, and deliberated on that knowledge. With Conquest gone, the gang was without a leader. Without a leader, the gang might fall apart or at the very least go back to their inefficient, haphazard running of the city. A gang with no purpose would not help further the cause. They needed a new leader and someone souled would cause the most theological damage.

On Earth for a week, it was time he did something proactive instead of playing catch up. Research was great. It told him who his allies were at all the military bases across Canada, but knowing who could help him didn't do much if he didn't act.

Furthering Conquest's mission helped his own. He closed the document, locked his computer, grabbed the keys for the armoury of out his top drawer, and grinned. It had been far too long since he'd been able to run rampant in a campaign. This one would not fail.

He left his office and walked the corridors of the base, adjusting the input to the surveillance cameras as he went with the flick of his hand. In front of the armoury, he glanced both ways down the shadowy corridor, reached out with his senses. Satisfied he was alone, he used the key and unlocked the door.

He went straight for the assault rifles and handguns. Using a cart he found just inside the door, he piled boxes of weapons and ammunition onto it. When the cart was full, he locked the door again and pushed it to a door on the other side of the base where his car waited.

Once all the weapons were stacked in his trunk, he climbed into his car and sped off. The second he was a hundred feet away from the base, the cameras would start working properly again, instead of showing the loop of empty corridors he'd been feeding them while he worked.

The drive to the Grange headquarters wasn't far, and he pulled in front of the warehouse fifteen minutes later. He'd changed out of his military uniform well after his shift ended, and the jeans, T-shirt, and heavy coat he now wore, while comfortable, didn't feel right. Of course, he couldn't drive up with a cache of weapons wearing his uniform. But he hated civilian clothing.

He banged on the door, prepared for suspicion. Surely someone would be attending to the place at such a late hour. Electricity hummed through wires overhead, accompanying the scurrying sounds of mice.

After a few moments, the click of a lock turning joined the night's sounds. The heavy door swung open and a bleary- eyed young man squinted at him, weapon levelled at Gunther's chest.

"What the fuck, man? Do you have a death wish?"

War raised his hands and backed away. "Sorry. Don't shoot. I have a delivery for Caleb Bishop."

The man stood straighter. "What kind of delivery?"

"Are you Caleb?" Based on Conquest's description of the man, he knew the person brandishing the gun was Caleb. He wanted to know if the man would admit to his identity.

"Who's asking?"

"Gunther. I bring a delivery from Victor."

"Victor, huh? He's in jail, or haven't you been reading the papers these days?"

"I do know. He arranged this delivery before going to jail. I'm his brother."

"He didn't mention having a brother." The man's brow wrinkled and he took a step closer.

"Indeed, he has three brothers. Are you Caleb?"

Without lowering the gun, the man leaned against the doorjamb and peered outside. "What's the delivery?"

"I can't tell you that unless you're Caleb."

"Ya, man. I'm Caleb. Now what's the delivery?"

A small group of three other members crowded behind Caleb, moving back and forth, trying to see what was going on. Murmurs filtered through about sleep, shooting him, taking his car.

Caleb squared his shoulders, turning around. "Shut up, man. This guy says he has a delivery from Victor. Stay here while I go check it out. Keep him covered."

As Caleb stepped out of the building, the other men raised guns at Gunther. He grinned at their naivety. Mere mortal weapons wouldn't hurt him, but they didn't know that.

At the car, Gunther pressed the button on his fob to open the trunk. A soft click sounded and the trunk popped up a few centimetres. Gunther yanked it wide-open.

Caleb let out a low whistle. "How many weapons do you have in there?"

"Enough to tide you over for a while. Until my brother comes back."

"Comes back?" Caleb rubbed a hand across his jaw.

"You didn't think a little jail would keep him away from his duties for long, did you?"

Determination flashed in his eyes. "No, of course not. He's coming back."

Gunther could practically see the plan forming in Caleb's mind as the man chewed on the knowledge that Victor would return. If Conquest's apprentice wanted to lead the gang, he'd need to do something drastic. And soon.

Caleb waved his hand for the other members of the gang to come out and help him with the weapons. Once they'd all been transferred to the gang's headquarters, War got into the vehicle.

"Put them to good use." He drove away, watching in his rear-view mirror as the gang members returned inside and secured the door.

Now that Conquest's mission was back in motion, there was other work to be done. War needed to find a hacker.

Chapter Two

The next day, Becky sat at her desk in the office she shared with Kevin Moore. A twinge of guilt stabbed her every time she came to work and saw his desk across from hers. The magic she'd used to insert herself into the life of a reporter took away his anchor status. But she was convinced it was for the greater good. When they realized they were going to be here for a while, helping humans, she needed something that would put her in the thick of things. How much more involved could a reporter get? They were the city's eyes, ears, and conscience.

When they realized they had to stop the apocalypse, her position at the TV station became even more important. With connections to law enforcement, politicians, and celebrities, she had information at her fingertips that might help roll the end of the world back. Demoting Kevin to co-anchor for the six o'clock news and giving him the late-night news spot was a small price to pay.

She picked up her coffee and took a sip, frowning at the tepid liquid. Before realizing everything she used her magic on might drain her power completely, she might have given the cup a little zap to warm her coffee. Instead, she took a large gulp, cringing at the coolness. Caffeine was still caffeine. Hot or cold, it would give her the energy she needed to analyze her spreadsheet.

She opened the document, filling in the details of the night before. If they were going to purposely get their power back, they needed to know what deeds increased their magic and which ones, if any, depleted it. As she inserted the information from yesterday, her gaze scanned the other cells. While she got no power back from helping out at the soup kitchen and nothing from saving the pawnshop owner by calling 911, she got some back saving a cat. And more back, once, when she paid for pizza.

With the new details input, she saved the spreadsheet and closed it again. There would be time later to analyze it and clearly she needed more information in order to figure it out.

Frustrated, she shoved the spreadsheet and her lack of power out of her mind. They were all smart angels and would figure it out eventually, but right now she had a pile of work on her desk and a keen desire not to be stuck in the office past her on screen broadcast for the evening news.

She picked up the pile of folders on her desk, shuffling through them, hoping one would pique her interest. But none of them did. The story about the gang wars and her mysterious tipster vied for her attention. She could work on both of those, vetting the tips as much as possible, maybe calling Rachel for help with the phone records. Though she hated calling her sister for assistance, it might be her only option.

She eyed her desk phone, ignoring the messages in a neat pile beside the base. Despite not wanting to inflate

Rachel's already impressive ego for picking the *right* job, she had no choice.

With a resigned grumble, she picked up the phone and called the police station, inputting Rachel's extension when prompted.

"Detective Malak." Rachel's crisp, no-nonsense voice greeted her.

"Hey, Rach. How are you doing?"

"What do you want, Beck?"

Becky sighed. "Can't I call my sister to find out how she's doing?"

Becky glanced through her office door to see if anyone was paying attention to her conversation. No one was. Everyone was too busy getting the evening's stories together, researched, planned, for them to notice or even care about what she was doing or who she was talking to.

The crackling sound of shuffling papers came over the phone line. "You can, but you never do. What's up? I'm kind of busy."

"Fine." Becky gritted her teeth and took a deep breath. "I was wondering if I could bring my phone by the station to see if your tech guys could learn anything about the blocked number that has been sending me tips."

"Interesting. You need my help."

"Yes. Can I bring it in?"

Rachel blew out a breath on the other end. Becky pictured a grin of satisfaction on her face. "Sure. Bring it over whenever you have some time. I know how hard you work there."

The sarcasm dripped out of the receiver. Instead of asserting the statement to be true and rising to Rachel's bait, Becky nodded. "Good. I'll bring it in this week."

"Preferably soon after they've texted another tip. It will make it easier for the tech guys to find something."

"Thanks."

She ended the call before either of them could get the other riled up some more. Rachel was able to push her buttons so easily. Maybe because Rachel was the oldest and thought they should all be as tough as she was.

As Becky picked up a thick folder about the gang activity in the city, Laura, her intern, breezed into the room. Her blond hair was pulled into her signature bun, with a few tendrils of hair framing her heart-shaped face. Sunken blue eyes, with smudges underneath, sparkled when she looked at Becky. She held a pile of small papers in her hand.

"Good! You're here. I have more messages for you."

With a yawn, she offered the stack to Becky. Suppressing a groan, Becky took them and added them to the already huge stack beside the phone. There weren't enough hours in the day to return them all.

"Thanks. Anything else?"

The woman's eyes lit up as she sank into the chair in front of Becky's desk. "I found someone who still has some vials of the flu vaccine. They fell down the back of the fridge at the clinic where they work. She's going to bring them over later today."

Becky leaned forward, her heart picking up speed. Something to investigate. Something to analyze. Something to sink her teeth into. If there was a problem with the vaccine, they would need someone to look into it. Her vaccine knowledge went as far as knowing they existed and created antibodies in the body.

"We'll need an expert in vaccines to look at it. There has to be something different about it this year."

Laura stood. "I'm on it."

"Wait!"

Becky opened the bottom drawer of her desk and

pulled out her purse. She dug into the side pocket and withdrew a ten-dollar bill.

"A tip?" Laura grinned.

"Get yourself a latte from the coffee shop around the corner. Looks like you could use a pick-me-up."

"Thanks. The usual for you?"

Becky nodded. "And let me know as soon as you've found an expert to look at that vaccine."

When Laura was gone, Becky turned back to the pile of work on her desk. A quick perusal of the messages confirmed they could wait for now, at least until lunch. Nothing urgent popped out at her. And if she was being honest with herself, the only messages that could snag her attention were ones about the gang, or another tip from her anonymous source. But they hadn't, so far, used a land-line or voice mail to impart information. It had all been through cryptic texts so far.

She opened up her task list application and added items to it that she needed to follow-up on. "Victor's" bail, the peace talks, gang activity. All a lull before the storm, especially with War likely here already. Heart racing, a rock formed in her stomach.

She pulled out her phone and opened the notes application. She typed in War??? If she could circle it, she would have done that too. They needed to figure out who he was. If he was here, there was no clue as to who he was or where he'd situated himself. No matter where he was, he would have magic on his side. That meant she had to figure out how she and her sisters could get their power back, fast.

Caleb Bishop stalked the conference room in front of the large screen at the front of the room, waiting for the other members of the gang to arrive. He'd summoned them all, but based on the snickers he received, he doubted many would show up. He would record the no-shows and they'd be dealt with accordingly after the coup.

The weapons from Gunther had been a help, shown he had connections, but it wasn't enough for them to respect him as leader. For that, he would need to do something drastic. And that would take patience. The gang didn't have a million dollars to bail Victor out of jail. Not that they would pay even if they had it. Somehow, he needed to find someone willing to spring the boss. The only way he could become head honcho was to destroy the current kingpin. And the gang needed a leader. They were falling apart with Victor in jail.

He checked his phone. Gang members had five more minutes to show up to his meeting or face the consequences. They had no idea what those consequences would be, but their lack of respect so far indicated they wouldn't take him seriously.

He stopped pacing and stood at the front of the room, back straight, arms loosely at his sides. He set the phone on the table, on a stand with the camera pointed forward. With a few swipes of the screen, he found his surveillance app and tapped the icon. He set it to take pictures at ten-second intervals so he could keep track of who showed up and what their facial expressions were as he talked.

One minute after the designated start time, Chris and Manny strolled into the room. They gave him a nod and slumped into chairs at the back of the room. Seconds later, Domenic, Pete, and Nick ambled into the area, choosing seats closer to the front. They sat, promptly swivelling to face Chris and Manny. A raucous chat ensued about weapons, the state of the prostitution business, how many drug deliveries they had to make later that day.

Caleb waited for more members to show up, checking the clock on the wall at the back to see how late everyone else was. Finally, ten minutes after the time the meeting was supposed to start, he cleared his throat. A few more members had trickled in, but he was still missing at least half of the group. Some were in the field doing the gang's work and would be forgiven for not attending. But the rest would be noted and dealt with. They could always recruit more members.

Conversation still flowed, louder than a few minutes earlier. He cleared his throat again. Getting no response, heat rushed to his face. He banged his fist on the table. The room fell silent, and everyone turned their chairs to face the front.

Domenic burst into laughter. "Man, no one is afraid of you. You're no one around here. Without Victor here, we can kick your ass out. Who's going to protect you now?"

Flashes of his father saying similar words to him, right before a punch to Caleb's face, went through his head. He took a deep breath, flared his nostrils, and marched over to the group of members on the left side of the table. The chuckling lingered.

Faster than any of them realized, he grabbed Chris's hair, shoved his head down, and smashed it against the table. Blood spurted onto the dark wood from the man's broken nose.

Domenic and Manny leapt to their feet.

Caleb stood his ground, legs equal distance apart, hands up, fists ready. His heart raced. Heat flushed his face. He wished he had a gun, but he remembered Victor's insistence that guns made you look weak. Fear the man, not the weapon. And they *would* fear him.

"You want to mess with me? Back off. Victor took me under his wing and I'm going to finish what he started with turning this gang around. You want to take that up with him when he gets out?"

Domenic backed away, hands raised in front of his chest. Manny followed suit, shaking his head. "No, man. You do what you want."

Caleb's heart still thundered in his chest. He clenched his hands at his sides and took a deep breath. He nodded to Pete. "Take him to the infirmary."

Everyone moved to do his bidding, but he pointed to the others. "Sit down. Text everyone else and tell them to join us if they're not out working the streets. They'll show if they don't want to join Chris in the infirmary."

The remaining members pulled out their phones, fingers flying over the screens to send messages. When Victor renovated the place to make the new gang head-quarters, he'd included everything a growing enterprise would need. Conference room, gym, lounge, small offices that had a bed and mini fridge in each one, kitchen area for a break room, and a wellness room for patching up members when they needed it. The only thing he hadn't done was get a doctor on staff. Maybe that would come later.

Once Chris and Pete were gone, Caleb marched back to the front of the conference room again. Never show them fear. He stayed there, with his back turned to the other members on purpose, waiting to see if they would attack. Unless he did something drastic, soon, he would lose the security he had. He would end up looking over his shoulder every waking moment, knowing the rest of the gang had it in for him. None of the members embraced his presence. They tolerated him while Victor was there because the leader said they had to. But with Victor gone, Caleb's hold over them was tenuous.

Shuffling noises and the creak of the conference room door prompted him to turn around. More members trickled into the room, taking up most of the remaining seats at the table.

Every person in the room sat, backs rigid, hands folded on top of the table, gazes directed at him.

"Good. You can fill in the rest of the gang when they get back."

He pierced each member with a hard stare and waited for them to look away before moving on to the next person. Some, like Domenic, lasted longer than others. It would be an uphill fight to convince them to follow him.

"As you can see, I have connections when it comes to weapons." He refused to tell them he had no idea how he had that connection. For whatever reason, Victor told his brother to deal with Caleb. For that, he was thankful. How long that weapons connection would sway the gang, he had no idea. The gang wasn't just about weapons. They were a full-service enterprise.

"I'll be taking over until Victor comes back. I have nothing to lose here. If you're with me, fortune and gratitude are in your future. If you're against me, pain and suffering. Choose wisely."

Grumbling filled the room, with a few distinct words of acquiescence filtering through. It would do for now. Some of the tension drained out of his shoulders. His mouth went dry. How long would the cooperation last?

"Good. Get back to work."

The longer Victor was away, the faster the members would rebel against Caleb. Other members were better suited to taking over as leader. All of them had been in the gang longer, committed more crimes, were tougher than he was. But he wanted it more. Wanted it so much he could taste it.

The easiest way to get their respect and become the leader of the gang was to kill Victor. But he couldn't do that with the man in jail. And none of them had the money to pay his bail. All the protection money, cuts from the sex workers, and drug money wouldn't be enough to have Victor released. At least not anytime soon.

When the last of the members filed out of the room, Caleb sank into the chair in front of the presentation screen, his mind whirling with questions.

For now, he was safe. The office he'd picked in the warehouse had a lock on the inside. He hadn't gone back to the apartment he'd lived in with his father for over a week now. The old man probably didn't even care, except now he had to do everything for himself. And he had no punching bag anymore.

He'd deal with that problem eventually too. He wanted his things, what little he had. When the time was right, he would take care of his father and become the official leader of the Grange.

After a long day at work, Becky sat in the loft she shared with Rachel, Sarah, and Leah, propped at the kitchen island, laptop open, scouring the internet for more signs of the apocalypse. Her back ached, the small throb insistent, urging her to get off her stool and stretch. But she didn't have time. They didn't have time. They'd been exiled from Heaven, not at the beginning of an apocalypse, but in the middle. Maybe even closer to the end, when the Earth was doomed, unable to pull itself out of the catastrophe human kind had created. With little time to at least halt the progress of the end of the world, she researched whenever she had some time.

Aromas of garlic, jasmine, and ginger teased her nose. Her stomach grumbled. Sarah was in the kitchen, making dinner like she always did if they weren't at Baron's. Staying in was a rare occasion for them. They preferred the ambiance, the music at Baron's while they worked on the apocalypse at hand.

Rachel sat on the living room sofa, pointing a remote at the television. She flipped through channels, finally stopping on the twenty-four-hour news station. A twinge of guilt crept up Becky's spine. Kevin Moore, in reality the more senior anchor, was stuck doing the eleven o'clock news when by rights, she should still be an intern. Once the apocalypse was over, she'd have to make it up to him. If she had most of her angelic gifts back, maybe she could pick a new life for herself, if she decided to stay on Earth, and give him back the one he should have had.

Giving in to the pain in her back, Becky hopped off the stool and walked across the open concept loft, through the living room, to the floor-to-ceiling windows that provided a spectacular view of the city. Fat, fluffy flakes gently drifted downward, dusting everything with a white powder. With the glow from the streetlights reflecting off the snow, the city looked serene. Not at all like a place where countless crimes happened every day.

She walked back to the kitchen and climbed up on her stool again. A hint of scallion wafted across the kitchen and she inhaled deeply. No matter what Sarah cooked, it always tasted amazing. Becky's stomach grumbled again.

"When is dinner going to be ready?"

Leah launched off the armchair in the living room and ran to the kitchen. "Can I help?"

Sarah chuckled. "Dinner will be ready when it's ready."

She looked at Leah. "Sure. Can you zest those limes?" Sarah nodded at the three limes on the counter.

While Leah went to work being a chef's assistant, Becky pulled up an article about locusts. She clicked the button on her browser to cast the screen to the TV.

Rachel sat up straighter. "Hey, I might have been watching that."

Becky raised an eyebrow. "Were you?"

Rachel slumped back into the cushions. "No. What have you learned about the signs?"

"Lots of weather phenomena that I'll get into later. This one caught my attention, though." She scrolled through the article slow enough for everyone to read it. "Does it count as a plague of locusts if a plane's cargo door that was carrying the insects for study ripped off and they fell out?"

Rachel tapped her foot. "Probably. Shit."

"Rachel," Becky admonished. Not that it would do any good.

"We've been over this. I swear. Especially when shit like that is happening." She gestured at the TV.

"Then you're not going to like the next one. Day turning to night."

Sarah walked over to the island to grab the salt and pepper. "There have been no eclipses."

Becky shook her head and pulled up another article. "No, but volcano eruptions with so much soot and ash that it will block out the sun for days in Iceland."

Sarah went back to the stove and seasoned the chicken. "When did that happen?"

Becky clicked the button to cast the new article to the television. "This morning. Based on the modelling, the particles will remain in the air over Iceland for at least three days."

"Plague, blotting out the sun, we can handle that." Rachel picked up her drink from the coffee table and took a long swallow.

"Maybe." Becky closed the articles and pulled up weather data from Environment Canada. "We've also got tornadoes where we don't usually get them. And earthquakes in regions that aren't even on tectonic zones."

"Did you get that information from your meteorologist? I doubt you actually dug all that up." Rachel leaned back into the sofa cushions, a smug look on her face.

Heat rose to Becky's cheeks. "Why do you do that?"

Rachel shrugged. "Am I right?"

Becky's pulse quickened. "What does it matter? The data still says apocalypse."

Sarah looked over her shoulder at them while she stirred the sauce on the stove. "Stop it, you two."

"I know I'm right."

Leah sighed. Becky ignored Rachel's triumphant glare and turned her attention to the youngest of them. "What's wrong?"

Leah shrugged, shaking her head. "Nothing really. Just a little jealous that you all fell together and I was last. You guys had three weeks to bond without me."

Memories flashed in Becky's mind of Leah, the youngest sister, tagging along all the time, not wanting to be left out. And Rachel, Sarah, and Becky doing everything they could to ditch her. It's what sisters did when three were so close in age, and the last one was a few years younger.

The memories were false but felt real enough, all to give them the sister bond. As much as they fought, like real sisters did, they loved each other. That's what the memories were supposed to foster. They also worked to give Leah the same sense of outsider syndrome as a youngest sister might feel.

Other memories flashed through her mind. Ones of Rachel always being right and always being smug about it. In all the memories that had been planted, not one of them showed Rachel admitting she was wrong, even when she was wrong.

Sarah, even in the memories, was a nurturer. Patching them up when they fell out of trees or off their bikes.

Would they have been friends when they were human, if they'd lived at the same time?

The only thing that was blurry in all the memories were their parents. Though they'd created a fiction around who their mother and father were, she couldn't form a picture of them in her mind. And no pictures of their parents sat on any of their desks or in their offices.

Sarah walked over to Leah, who was now finished zesting the limes, and gave her a side hug. "Sit at the breakfast island. You're here now and we love you. Don't we?"

Sarah looked at Becky, then pointedly at Rachel.

Becky nodded. "Of course we love you."

Rachel sighed. "Yes. Still not sure how a teacher is going to help stop the apocalypse, though."

"Rachel!" Becky shot the oldest sister a piercing look.

"What? Sisters harass each other, don't they?"

"You're like a dog with a bone." Becky closed the article and stopped casting to the TV.

Leah took a seat on a stool that faced the living room. "Knowledge is power." She pointed to her head. "Since nothing leaves this thing I'm sure I'll be instrumental in figuring it out."

When Leah had been alive, she'd had an eidetic memory. Now that she was an angel, she retained that ability, making Becky a little jealous. It would be a great skill to have as a reporter. Remembering and being able to recall all the information she'd read for researching her stories.

"Dinner's ready," Sarah said.

The clink of dishes and the ding of cutlery filled the kitchen as Sarah set the island for dinner. Rachel pushed herself up from the sofa and sat beside Becky facing the kitchen.

Sarah put the components of the meal on the table so they could assemble their dish themselves. Jasmine rice, naan bread, chicken in a savoury sauce. With cilantro, sour cream, and green onions in separate small bowls for garnish.

"We can look into the apocalypse later. Now, eat," Sarah said.

Becky closed her laptop and put it on the coffee table in the living room. As she sat on her stool again, her phone pinged.

"That can wait," Sarah warned.

"It can't. I just need to check it."

Becky picked up her phone and pressed the home key to display the notifications. Another text from her anonymous source flashed on the screen.

What's wrong with the flu vaccine?

X

Chapter Three

Wednesday morning, Father Ianetti adjusted his collar as he walked toward the hefty guard behind the desk. All visitors to the prison had to sign in and he'd thought about what he would say his reason for being there was. It wasn't every day he went to visit someone in prison. Since the death penalty had been abolished in 1976, many priests still had occasion to come to a jail or prison to council an inmate and now it was his turn. In precise, neat script, he wrote his reason for visiting - prisoner requested confession. Of course he didn't know if Victor had even made a phone call, but he had a story to get around that as well should his reason be questioned.

After signing in, he followed the guard to a heavy metal door with thick bars, spaced evenly apart. There was barely room between the bars for a child's arm, let alone a grown man's. A loud buzz made him jump. The guard yanked the door aside and waved his hand.

"Follow me."

Father Ianetti nodded and followed the guard. At another door, he waited for it to be opened, this time prepared for a buzz to unlock it. The heavy metal door swung open and Father Ianetti peered into the spacious room used for visiting with prisoners. Grey, cracked walls, faded with age, lent a depressing air to the room. Chairs, bolted to the floor, sat in front of metal tables. He settled into one that the guard indicated and placed his hands on top. The cold metal sent a shiver through him.

"Don't give anything to the prisoner and don't accept anything from the prisoner."

Father Ianetti nodded. The guard left, the keys at his side jingling as he walked. Another guard brought Victor into the room, nudging him to sit down in front of Father Ianetti.

The man sitting in front of him looked like Conquest. Tall, confident, with the same tattoo on his arm. But there was something different about this person. Father Ianetti leaned forward and took a deep breath. Fire and brimstone were missing. There was no scent of hell or decay on the man. Had jail changed him somehow? He'd heard stories about how being on the inside changed a man, but did it affect them that deeply and that fast? Father Ianetti leaned back.

"How are you doing?" A conversation with him might shed some light on the changes.

Victor smiled and the gesture appeared genuine. Another clue that this was not the Conquest the priest had summoned. "Fine. Itching to get out of here. You paying my bail?"

Father Ianetti guffawed. "The church can't afford that."

Even if his parish could afford such a high bail, the church would not, on the record, bail out a known gang leader. And he was almost sure this was not the person he was supposed to be, though he couldn't explain why.

Victor crossed his arms over his chest. "Then why are you here?"

Indeed. Why had he come? To see if Conquest could do anything from jail to further the plan. But he couldn't ask this man that question.

"I came to see how you're doing. Can't be easy being cooped up in here." He stopped himself from saying too much. The guards were always listening. There would be no expectation of privacy in the visiting area of a prison. Other visitors and prisoners could overhear conversations at neighbouring tables.

Father Ianetti glanced around the room, taking in the other occupants. A woman with red eyes and a blotchy face shredded a napkin. The stern-looking man in front of her softened his gaze and reached across the table, coming just short of touching her hand. He glanced over his shoulder at the guard and pulled his hand back as if burned.

Other tables were loud. Boisterous. And still others, quiet, as the people stared at each other across the table, unwilling to be the first to speak.

Father Ianetti gazed into Victor's eyes, leaning forward again to get a closer look. Out of the corner of his eye, he spotted the guard walking closer.

Father Ianetti backed away. Prison hadn't changed Conquest. The person in front of him was not the horseman.

"Whoever did this"—he waved at Victor in a circular motion—"did a great job. But you're not him."

Victor laughed, the booming sound making people at the next table jump. "Sure I am. Have the attempted shank in the gut to prove it."

Father Ianetti shook his head. No, he wasn't the real Conquest. And that put a serious wrench in his plans. All the horsemen needed to be present for his plan to work.

The apocalypse couldn't happen if he was one horseman short. He didn't know how this person came to be, but he knew one thing for sure. He needed to summon Conquest again.

Becky sat at her desk at the TV station, shuffling through the myriad stories vying for her attention. She couldn't get to all of them, so she clicked the icon to create a new email message, typed a quick note, attached all the soft copy information she had, and sent the email to Laura. If her intern couldn't fit it in, Laura would delegate to another intern. That was something Becky had told her to do the moment they started working together. At least Laura would remember it that way. They'd only been working together a little shy of two months.

About to fire off another email, a new message popped up in her inbox. From the name attached to the message, it was from the expert Laura had found. A flush of adrenaline made Becky's body tingle. She loved this part of a story. The investigation, gathering of information, talking to experts. Curious as to what he could have found so soon, she clicked to open the email.

Disappointment settled in her stomach like a lead balloon as she scanned the message. He wanted to talk in person. Did that mean he had information or not? Maybe he wanted more information before he could comment on the sample Laura had sent over. They'd given him everything they could already.

She clicked to forward the email, put Laura's name in the to field, then paused. Laura already had a lot on her plate, and it was likely that the expert would want to speak with Becky, instead of an intern. She clicked to close the email and selected no when prompted to save to draft.

She fired off an email agreeing to a meeting. If he didn't get back to her right away, she would call to set something up. The longer they waited to confirm the anonymous tip, the longer it would take for the story to come together. She needed to show her producer something soon so they could start running promos for the series.

An email popped into her inbox. He wanted to see her as soon as possible. Instead of messaging back, she grabbed her purse from the bottom drawer of her desk, yanked her coat off the hook behind the door, and scurried out of her office. The lab where he worked wasn't far away. If she pretended she was a speed walker, she could get there in under ten minutes.

Upon arriving at the lab, as she reached for the thick glass door, a tingling sensation passed over her wings. She gasped, smiled. Inside, she raced over to the reception desk and asked for Dr. Adil Karimi's office. The man at the reception pointed to a bank of elevators on her right.

"Is there a restroom down here?"

He nodded and pointed to the left to another bank of elevators. "End of the elevators and then a left."

She didn't have time to check, but she couldn't help wanting confirmation now. It had taken so long to get more power back in her wings, she wanted to make sure it wasn't simply another December breeze teasing her feathers.

In the ladies' room, she checked every stall to make sure she was alone. She shrugged out of her coat, unfurled her wings, and grinned like a toddler with a new toy at the new white patch in the middle of the left limb. She made a note to add this to her spreadsheet when she returned to the office. Once she had time to analyze the events, maybe she would figure out what actions rewarded her with more power.

Five minutes later, after a wait for an elevator car, she pushed through the doors of Queen City Research Group. Not generally open to the public, there was no receptionist, so she had to flag someone down as they walked by. Absorbed in their tablet, a petite woman wearing a crisp white lab coat almost bumped into her.

"Could you tell me where Dr. Karimi is?"

The woman's eyebrows pinched together when she looked up. "Sorry, yes, he's over there by the window."

The space was divided into three sections. Straight ahead were cubicles for doing analyses, she assumed. And based on what she saw when someone came out a door on the right, right and left were doors leading to hallways with labs.

She meandered over, casually glancing at desks and computers as she walked. When she approached, he looked up, a smile of recognition crossing his face.

The smile grew to Cheshire cat proportions and he thrust out a hand to shake hers.

"This is a nice surprise. When I said I wanted to meet, I assumed your intern would be following up."

"It's nice to meet you, Dr. Karimi. Laura has a lot of other stuff on her plate. I keep her pretty busy. You wanted to tell me something about the vaccine?"

He gestured to a stool in front of a metal table. A multitude of lab equipment took up the table, with a small patch near the edge left empty save for a mug with a pun about rocket science.

Becky perched on the edge of the stool. Dr. Karimi peered into a microscope, frowned, and glanced at her.

"This sample has a slightly different make up than

previous flu vaccines, but nothing jumps out at me. It could have been that they used more strands of the virus than previous vaccines. Or less. It would need further testing."

"That would be great. Whatever you can find out will help."

"I'll contact a microbiologist I know to look into it further. Her name is Dr. Isolde Althaus."

"Thank you. Will you get back to me as soon as you hear anything?"

"Of course. What is this all about? Is there something wrong with the vaccine?"

"I can't say much. I'm following a lead. Plus, I don't want to bias you in any way, to look in a certain direction. Anything you can find out about the vaccine will help."

"You're a smart cookie. I will reach out to my contact and get back to you as soon as I know more."

She thanked him and dashed out of the lab. Instead of waiting for the elevator, she raced down the stairs, bursting into the lobby winded but exhilarated. Her heart pumped faster, and she paused to take a few deep breaths. Another tingle settled over her wings. Familiar with what that meant, she didn't rush to the bathroom this time, but made a note to add this to her spreadsheet as well.

On her way back to the TV station, she stopped at Rachel's work at Adelaide and University. Heavy glass doors gave pedestrians a glance into the building, but Rachel's department wasn't on the main floor.

Becky waltzed in, nodded to the constable at the desk, and beelined directly to the elevators. They knew her here and she rarely had any trouble going up to the floor where the detectives did their work unless a rookie manned the desk.

She headed straight for Rachel's desk, hoping her sister was still in the office. It was possible she was out chasing leads, interviewing suspects, for whatever new cases had popped up since yesterday. Toronto was a big city and the detectives always had some sort of major crime to investigate.

When she rounded a corner, tension drained from her shoulders at the sight of Rachel sitting at her desk, head bent, looking over something.

Becky sat in the chair beside Rachel's desk and placed her cell phone on top of the page Rachel was perusing. Rachel scowled at her but snatched up the phone.

"We can drop it off with the tech guys on the way to the break room."

Becky followed Rachel down a hallway, then they left the phone with a bespectacled woman who barely looked up when they walked in. She grunted a reply when Rachel asked her to tag it for incoming texts and calls.

In the break room, Becky munched on a tuna sandwich, periodically checking her pocket for her phone. Not used to being without it for more than a few minutes, the phantom buzzing annoyed her.

"It's a phone. It's not like..."

"Like what? Like I have real work to do?"

Rachel shrugged, leaned back in her chair, and popped a potato chip into her mouth. "You said it, not me."

"Why do you have so much resentment for my job?"

She shrugged again. "Sorry. I'm trying to be better. Getting information to the people is important. I acknowledge that. When they're ready to hear it."

Before Becky could prompt her further, Rachel's phone rang.

"Your phone is ready."

They rushed back to the lab, both of them eager for Becky to go back to her own place of work. The tech's glasses were now perched on top of her head. She handed the phone over to Becky.

"The last text came in from a burner phone. I put an app on the phone to trace the next one, but it won't be able to get the number. May only be able to triangulate the general area it was sent from. All I could make out is that it is coming from an 825 area code."

Becky pulled up a search app on her phone and plugged in the area code.

"That's in Alberta," Becky said. "Thanks. You've been a big help." She turned to Rachel. "See you at home."

She needed to get back to the office to see what the heck was in Alberta.

———

In the loft that evening, Becky sat in the living room on the sofa, a mug of tea losing heat on the coffee table in front of her. Tabs open in her internet browser ranged from peace talks to Alberta phone numbers. She hadn't found anything in Alberta that pointed to why someone would be texting her about a flu vaccine. The peace talks research was worse. There was talk about moving them if they didn't make progress. Anger was running high on both sides and war would likely be the result if the facilitators couldn't get both sides to take a deep breath and calm down.

Leah sat in the plush chair facing the floor-to-ceiling window, plugging away with research into what they needed to send War back to limbo. The consensus was the horseman was already here, and the peace talks would fail.

Cracking her knuckles, she wanted to shake the priest they believed responsible for summoning the horsemen. It was obvious he wasn't a true vessel of God's message. How could he think this was the best way to handle fixing the Earth?

The scents of savoury garlic and pungent onion drifted in from the kitchen, making her stomach grumble. Sarah was making dinner. It was unusual for them to be sequestered in the loft, but on this cold evening, it was nice staying in. The world seemed so quiet, so at peace under a blanket of fresh snow.

A presence over her shoulder made her frown.

"Not handing it all off to your intern?"

Becky bristled, turning to glare at Rachel. "I do my own work."

Rachel smirked. "Sometimes."

"And what are you doing right now?" Becky crossed her arms over her chest and stuck out her chin.

Her sister didn't have a laptop, just a drink. How much research was she going to get done using a cup of coffee?

Rachel plunked her mug onto the coffee table and crashed into the sofa like a car out of gas. There still wasn't a lot of white in Rachel's wings, so she hadn't been doing anything consistently to get her power back either.

"Must be tough still having so little power. But don't take it out on me."

Rachel gave her a side-eye. "I'm thinking about every-thing. War is obviously already here."

Leah nodded. "The breadcrumbs I'm finding will lead to answers. I'm sure of it."

"Do we still have enough supplies from sending Conquest back? Some of the ingredients for War must be the same."

From the kitchen, Sarah said, "Yes. The ingredients to summon him to us are almost the same for all the horse-men, except Death. One thing that differs is the sigil we burn so we get the horseman we want. We also have most of the ingredients for sending him back. Death requires a few extra ingredients to summon him."

Rachel pulled her legs under her and settled more comfortably into the sofa. "Speaking of Conquest, Victor had a visit from Father Ianetti."

"How do you know that?" Becky asked.

"A guard let me know. And that's proof the priest is at least part of the plot to bring about the apocalypse. I wish I could tell Williams all this. He still doesn't understand my distrust of the priest."

"Get your laptop and help us search. The sooner we find the spell and ingredients to send War back, the better. Maybe you won't have to explain everything to your partner if we can put a halt to the apocalypse."

Chapter Four

F ather Ianetti tapped his foot under his cassock and smiled until his cheeks hurt as he watched the last of his parishioners trickle out of the church after private prayer. Confessions ended over an hour ago, and he'd never been so tired and his voice so hoarse. The number of sinners coming to confess had jumped. Thanks to his sermons, they saw the truth. That the final days were approaching and the only way to secure their place in Heaven was through redemption. If any of them survived the end of the world, some of them might join the Holy Father in Heaven after their death.

He'd long ago resigned himself to Hell. For good to happen, bad things sometimes needed to be done. His pact with Lucifer and giving up his soul was a small price to pay for saving mankind. He would see all of his fellow Omega members in Hell. There would be casualties, of course. That couldn't be helped. Lots of casualties would ensure man came out of the battle stronger, hopefully smarter.

He nodded a farewell to his last parishioner, closed the heavy wooden church door, and locked it. Priding himself on his church always being a sanctuary, always open, this was the third time he'd locked the door in as many months. It couldn't be helped. The ritual he must perform needed to be done in private, with no interruptions. He'd sent the rest of the church staff home hours ago to make sure nothing would interfere with what needed to be done.

He shuffled through the nave, to the back of the church, through a side door that led to his room.

The black robe he needed was already laid out on his bed. Before he could wear it, he needed to purify his body. Drawn hours ago, the bath water would be cool, but not uncomfortably so.

He took off his clothes, folded them neatly, and placed them on the chair beside his bed. He walked into the small en suite bathroom and dipped a toe into the water. A shiver raced up his spine. Without hesitation, he sank his foot to the bottom and followed with the rest of his body. Submerged, he held his breath, the heavily salted water stinging his lips. Grit from the salt rubbed against his legs. When his head started to pound, he pushed himself out of the water and gasped for air. Standing, he pulled the stopper out of the tub.

He got out and dried quickly with a threadbare towel that barely soaked up the moisture. The robe stuck in spots as he put it on where the towel had left droplets of water.

With no time for dawdling, he rushed to the cabinet against the back wall of his room and pulled out the items he needed. Pure black, pillar candles, herbs, ritual knife, pewter bowl, lighter, the sigil he'd created—again. The other sigils for the remaining horsemen had been drawn months ago. This one was hastily drawn, not as precise, so he hoped it worked.

Items assembled, he raced out to the backyard. He'd marked the circle earlier in the day. No one used the backyard anymore, especially in winter, so he was sure it would be undisturbed.

A rectangular flat stone in the middle acted as an altar. He arranged the candles on the ground in a circle around the stone. In front of the candles, he placed the athame, his ritual knife, that he needed for all the rituals. He put the pewter bowl on top of the stone.

Taking a deep breath to brace himself against the cold, he removed the robe. He raised his arms over his head and called on the four corners of the Earth and the four elements. Once the circle was sealed, he lit the candles and recited the incantation. He repeated it over and over. Would it be harder this time, since someone had sent the horseman back to limbo?

Finally, he set the sigil alight, dropping it into the bowl. He pricked his finger and squeezed drops of blood into the ashes. He pleaded with the devil to grant his wish.

Minutes ticked by. A breeze chilled his skin. The air stilled. A suffocating heat overwhelmed him. Falling to the ground, he gasped for air, clutching his throat.

Wisps of white smoke in the shape of a horse appeared. It galloped past him. Out of thin air, Conquest popped into existence. Clothes automatically formed over his body.

"What took you so long? Those sisters sent me back. Fucking angels."

Father Ianetti bent to grab the robe and pulled it back on. "I wasn't aware until recently. You're supposed to be in jail. Angels sent you back?"

Conquest grinned. "I'll take care of it. Yes. They're going to be a problem."

"We'll deal with them if they get in our way. Your brother is here too."

"Where?" Conquest lifted his head and sniffed the air. "Never mind. Found him."

Before Father Ianetti could say another word, Conquest took off, bounding over the brick wall surrounding the backyard. Angels changed things. He needed to be prepared. Right now he was too tired to do anything but sleep. Tomorrow, after his sermons, he would make more sigils and stock up on ingredients to call the horsemen. The angels would not stop him, or Omega, from the mission.

The next morning, Conquest strolled into the armoury building on Centre Avenue to see War. He'd been sampling the air the entire time during his walk from his new digs to here. Since he could no longer pose as the leader of the Grange gang, he'd taken the persona of a business man a few blocks away from the church. The guy's condo was small, but with a view of the city that was woven into the price of the measly square footage. He didn't need much. Once the rest of his brothers arrived, they would be too busy to rest. And lucky for them, they didn't need sleep like mere mortals.

A private at the front desk looked up and smiled when he approached. She sat up straighter, her gaze following his every move. He didn't know what his brother's name was this time around. Since they could pick whatever they wanted when they were needed on Earth, War tended to pick something new each time.

He wracked his brain for the names War had used over the years, trying to determine what his name would likely be now.

"I'm here to see the guy in charge of the weapons."

Nothing came to him, so he went with the role he would play instead. There were numerous bases in Ontario. The armoury had been picked for a reason. Why pick an armoury, if you weren't going to be in charge of the place?

"Do you have an appointment?"

"He's expecting me. I'm his brother, Vic."

The woman's demeanour changed to one of relaxed confidence. "I'll let him know." She pressed a buzzer and War's voice replied to send him in.

She gestured to the now unlocked door behind her. "It's down that hall and then the first right to another hall. He's got an office at the end of that hallway."

Noting the cameras that saw everything, he opted to walk like a person instead of using power to get him to the office in a heartbeat. He knocked on the door with Major-General Gunther Fertig on a plaque and didn't bother waiting for an answer.

War sat behind a large desk, a frown of greeting on his face.

"What the hell happened?"

"Angels."

"Interesting. So, He thinks He can stop the apocalypse?"

Conquest shrugged. "He didn't open the seals, so I guess He does think that. Cocky too, because I'd bet on the famine that's approaching that they're fallen angels."

"Gotta love His positive attitude."

Conquest sank into a chair in front of the desk. "They had enough magic to send me back to limbo, but they aren't working at full power."

"That should help us."

Gunther went back to looking at something on his laptop.

"What are you doing?" Conquest fought the urge to

stand behind War. The horseman didn't like anyone on his flank.

"Finishing what you started."

He filled Conquest in about Caleb and the weapons.

"It would be great for the apocalypse if a souled person was the new leader of the gang." War regarded him with a challenging look.

"I'm on it. But Victor is in jail."

"I'm working on that right now. Hiring a hacker for future missions and about to get a demonstration."

War turned the computer sideways so Conquest could see the screen. A request for a test was already written in a draft email, asking to make it look like bail had been paid for Victor. War hit send.

"And now we wait."

A ping came back almost immediately with an affirmative response.

"He's eager, this hacker," Conquest said.

"With what I plan to pay him, he should be. We'll need him for planting trails later. If he knew the part he was going to play in the end of the world, I'm sure he would have asked for more money."

Over the internet, it was impossible to know whether the hacker had a soul or not. Based on Death's almost purge of purgatory, it was highly unlikely unless the hacker was in his late seventies or older.

Minutes later, the hacker sent another email, this one with an attachment. It was a copy of a receipt showing the bail as being paid.

"Perfect." Conquest stood.

There was work to be done, and a full briefing could happen later, once more plans were in motion. Another briefing would be needed once Famine and Death were here anyway.

Gunther turned the laptop back. "After you take care of the gang, I need you to get a job at a lab at the university."

"Consider it done."

He strolled out of the office, a smile turning up his lips. He missed being here. Missed the sickly sweet stench of the soulless. It filled the hallways, lingered in the streets, overpowered his condo. The angels would not be able to stop what was coming.

Becky sat at her desk, a mug of coffee slowly getting colder, shooting off research requests to the TV station's interns. Laura was already busy working with her on the anonymous tips, so she gave the others the background work for stories she would be reporting on early next week. As long as the work was done, Ellen didn't care who did the research. And Becky was too busy trying to stop the apocalypse to focus on stories that wouldn't bring her closer to her goal.

Laura sat across from her, in the chair closest to the door, flipping through file folders containing various aspects of the increased violence in the city story. That was the one piece that did align with the whole stopping the end of the world.

"Put that aside for now. I'm sure when a new leader for the Grange takes over, we'll know."

Rachel would tell her. After Detective Littman, the gang expert, told her.

"Great. Thanks. It was depressing. What do you want me to work on instead?"

Becky clicked through her tabs in her internet browser. "Can you look into vaccines and contagions? How vaccines are created, what growth mediums are used. Anything you can get me that doesn't require a Ph.D. to understand."

Laura nodded. "On it."

"And can you find out where Dr. Isolde Althaus works?"

She hadn't thought to ask Dr. Karimi at the time, but if he was forwarding her question, Dr. Althaus might reply to her directly. She didn't want to risk marking it as SPAM if that happened.

Her cell phone, face down on her desk, buzzed. Her heart raced. She picked it up, frowning at the cryptic message.

> Have you checked the BSL of vaccine creating labs?

> X

Frowning, Becky read the message five times.

"What's wrong?" Laura leaned closer to the desk, closing the lid of her laptop to get a look at Becky's phone.

Becky turned her cell phone to show Laura the screen.

"Can you find out if the lab Dr. Althaus works at creates vaccines?"

"Sure. You want me to research the biological safety levels too?"

Becky shook her head. "I'll do that. You have a lot on your plate."

A tingle went through Becky. Before she could dwell on the tingle, her phone buzzed again. This time it was a text from Sarah, reminding her they were having dinner at Baron's later.

Sarah was telling her about dinner, and she hadn't even had lunch yet. Her stomach grumbled and Laura laughed.

"I can run down to the cafeteria."

"That would be awesome."

Becky pulled open her bottom drawer, grabbed some bills, and gave them to Laura.

"Going to surprise me and have something different?"

Becky raised an eyebrow. "And get something for yourself."

"I'll find out about Dr. Althaus' employer first."

Laura hurried off. Becky leaned back in her chair, closed her eyes, and let her mind wander with all the questions she had about the tips. With Famine being the next horseman due to arrive, pestilence and pandemics weren't far behind. But her tipster was focused on the flu vaccine. Influenza was bad, sure. The last flu pandemic in 2010 had killed between 100,000 to 400,000 people worldwide. Since then, the infections and severity had dropped. What did the BSL of the labs that created the flu vaccine have to do with what was different about it?

Of course, with horsemen in the mix, anything was on the table when it came to the cause of a pandemic. Frustrated, she opened her eyes and stared at her email inbox.

An email from Laura told her Dr. Althaus worked at Queen City University Research Group. Under that, a new message from Dr. Karimi sat there, hopefully with answers to questions she didn't know she had.

She clicked on the email and scanned through the message from Dr. Karimi, frowning as the science got more complicated. She read through the email a few more times and was biting her lip when Laura returned with sandwiches.

"Problem?" Laura placed lunch on Becky's desk and took a seat.

"Dr. Karimi said Dr. Althaus looked at the genetic

sequence of the virus used in the vaccine and it encoded two components of the influenza virus."

The blank look on Laura's face made Becky feel better. "What does that mean? And what did it encode?"

Becky shrugged, took a bite of her sandwich, and chewed thoughtfully for a moment. "I guess it means it's not a full flu vaccine. I read somewhere that the vaccine is usually components of three or four flu strains. Or maybe something else got put in the mix by mistake."

"According to Dr. Karimi, Dr. Althaus says the other components are not normally seen in vaccines, but they are harmless and aren't doing anything, but could be why it wasn't as effective."

"Why haven't we heard about it not being as effective yet?" Laura took a sip of her pop.

"Good question. And why don't I believe her? If it was all harmless, why would someone be texting, urging us to look into the vaccine?"

"Maybe it's a disgruntled lab employee."

"Maybe."

Becky closed the message so she wouldn't be tempted to read it again. Despite the person being an expert, and apparently trusted by Dr. Karimi, she didn't trust what the woman said. A clenching in her stomach told her there was more to this than they knew so far.

She pulled up her browser and did a search for biosafety levels. Pages of information came back as a result. Too many for her to check them all, but the most relevant ones were on the first page. She clicked to read about the levels, and what kinds of diseases would be handled at each one.

"Laura, do we know where that vaccine was made?"

"The sample? It was out of the Queen City University

Research Group. They developed this year's vaccine for the country and exported some to the U.S."

"Interesting. That is where Dr. Althaus works. The fact that she's denying there's anything harmful about the vaccine doesn't hold any water now."

Abandoning the BSL search for the time being, Becky opened another tab and keyed in a search for QCURG. Based on the stated research engaged at the university lab, it should have a biosafety level of two.

Intuition punched her in the gut. After several searches, she finally hit on a search term that garnered results. She pulled up the document with the blueprints to the university's microbiology lab. Based on the design of the building, isolated from the rest of the research facility, underground, with a dedicated HVAC system, it looked to have a BSL of 4.

Why would they need the measures in place for BSL 4 if the most dangerous virus they worked on was the flu? Stumped and intrigued, Becky grabbed her phone and fired off a message back to the person asking for more information. Why were they being so cryptic in their tips?

It occurred to her the person might be watched all the time. Or maybe they didn't know any more than they were revealing through the messages. Maybe someone was feeding them information and they were passing it along.

She glanced at her phone, willing the person to message back with at least a morsel more, but nothing happened. Her phone didn't buzz. Did it even go through? What if they ditched their phone as soon as they sent the message? If they were using a new burner phone every time, that would add up to a decent expense.

Patience might be a virtue, but she wasn't feeling especially virtuous at the moment. She swiped the screen to unlock her phone and called Rachel's number at the police station.

"Hey, can you check to see who sent the last text to my phone? I just received another message a few minutes ago."

"Hang on. Corrie gave me the monitoring app to check."

The sound of Rachel's fingers clacking on the keyboard grated on Becky's nerves. She clenched her jaw and tapped her fingers on her desk while she waited for the results of Rachel's inquiry.

"No phone number. But it's still an 825 area code."

"Thanks. Did Sarah message you about dinner tonight?"

Rachel chuckled. "Yes. She's eager to try the new menu. Plus, she doesn't have to cook."

After she hung up, she did more searching on the internet. Beyond knowing the area code was in Alberta, she hadn't checked into it further. Laziness, or not enough time, prevented her from digging deeper. Now, she punched in the area code and waited for the results to pop up.

"The texts are coming from Alberta. And according to this, the area code overlays the entire province. So we can't even narrow it down to the north or south of the province."

"They're not making it easy, are they?" Laura asked.

"They are not." Becky finished her sandwich and took a gulp of her now cold coffee. She made a face and Laura laughed.

"You want another one?" Laura nodded to the mug.

Becky stood. "I'll top it up, maybe pop it in the microwave."

Not a coffee connoisseur, it didn't matter to her if the

beverage was reheated because it was half a day old. Most people would have finished drinking it by now, but she'd been too busy to drink.

She felt another tingle cascade over her wings. She plunked her mug down in the break area and raced to the bathroom. After quickly checking the stalls to confirm she was alone, she unfurled her wings. Another white patch had started to form near the tip of her right limb.

She did a little fist bump, then glanced over her shoulder to make sure she was still alone. At this rate, she might get all the power back by next week if she could find a pattern. Once she got back to her desk, she needed to spend a little time analyzing her wing data before tackling more information about the vaccine.

Sitting at the back of Baron's, Becky munched on a fry dipped in mayonnaise. The explosion of flavours in her mouth made her smile. One thing they all liked about being back on Earth was the food. Having to eat and sleep, while annoying, did have some pleasurable aspects. The other day, she'd even dreamed they'd been successful and were back home looking down over their good work.

The reality of the situation when she'd woken up had been disheartening but gave her added motivation to accomplish their mission. There had still been no confirmation from Him that they'd deduced correctly as to why they were here. With the current happenings, though, there could be no other reason.

Leah and Sarah sat with her, while Rachel was on a patrol around the place, looking for possible trouble. Since she'd put out a warning that the bar and the owner were to be left alone by all the gangs in the city, she frequently popped by even if they weren't staying for dinner, to make sure the ne'er-do-wells were abiding by her warning.

On a Thursday evening, the bar was packed. Rachel squeezed through patrons, letting out a huff when she plopped into her chair.

"Everything looks good from my perspective."

"My turn." Becky jumped out of her chair and started her own patrol. This time looking for souls.

Her circuit started at the back, along the wall, all the way to the front of the place, in front of the stage, then completing her circuit by walking up the other side along the bar. She was frowning when she returned to the table.

"Not good news?" Sarah snatched her hand away from Becky's plate with a few fries.

"There are only three people here tonight with souls. They're older, down at the front near the doors."

Rachel's phone buzzed. She glanced at it, a frown pulling her eyebrows together.

"What's wrong?" Becky sat up, swatting Sarah's hand away as the angel tried to snag another fry.

"Victor is out on bail. Shit."

"So much for having a source of light inside the jail." Becky took a bite out of her burger.

"We have to double down on figuring out who War is," Rachel said.

Leah pulled over an empty table to make their overall space larger. When they finished eating, they moved their plates to the empty table, then pulled out their laptops from their bags on the floor at their feet. They rarely went anywhere without them. Which made sense for her and Leah. She wasn't sure what excuse Rachel or Sarah would give if ever questioned as to why they had computers wherever they went.

"I bet the priest has summoned Conquest again too," Rachel said.

Becky nodded. "He probably won't go back to the gang, though. He might even look like someone else. At least to everyone else."

The glamour the horsemen used was powerful and would fool everyone they came into contact with. An angel, with power, would see the horseman as they really were, not the person they pretended to be. It had taken too long for them to figure out who Conquest was when he first arrived. He'd already done damage that might not be able to be undone.

Leah took a sip of her drink. "We need to figure out who they are, sooner rather than later."

Sarah raised a hand to get the waiter's attention. "I see much caffeine in our future."

Despite not being tired, Becky wanted the caffeine. It might help the cognitive flow and she liked the taste. It was going to be a long night.

Chapter Five

Conquest blended into the late afternoon shadows outside the Grange gang's headquarters, waiting for one of the members to stray from the herd. A group of them had just returned from "business" in the heart of the city. Caleb was in the centre of the group, surrounded by Tony, the gang's enforcer, and a few of the not so important lackeys. It had taken him longer than he'd wanted to slip away to help Caleb take over the gang. Other work needed to be done, though, and he needed to establish himself as a lab technician so he could follow through on War's request to get a job.

Everyone crowded around the entrance to the place but held back, letting Caleb enter first. Tony remained at the back, the protector, watching for signs of malicious intent from anyone who might be walking by.

Conquest crunched the brown grass under his feet with his boots. When that didn't work to get Tony's attention, Conquest bent to pick up a handful of rocks. He tossed them, one at a time, against the side of the building until Tony turned toward the noise.

Conquest smiled.

The enforcer wouldn't recognize him. Because of the impostor he'd had to take on a different visage. He stepped out of the shadows once all the other gang members had disappeared inside.

"Hey, you can't be here, buddy." Tony stalked over.

Conquest shrugged. "I need to be here."

Tony's pace increased, and Conquest was ready for the blow that sailed through the air. He blocked it easily. With a body shot, he hit Tony square in the stomach. An elbow to the back of the head knocked the hulking enforcer to the ground. He'd have a headache when he woke up, but he'd be alive. Killing him wouldn't do much good and the gang needed to increase their numbers, not decrease them.

He glamoured into Tony, affected the same swagger as the enforcer had, and marched into the headquarters.

He found most of the members in the conference room. Doppelgänger Victor stood at the front of the room, talking about their latest venture. It was a good likeness of him, almost convincing, except it was a bit mechanical in its actions. The speech pattern wasn't natural, not to mention a bit clipped. He doubted anyone would notice.

"So, Victor, it's great and all that you're back, man, but maybe you two should spar to see if you're still fit to lead." Conquest watched the eyes on the rest of the members' faces bulge in their sockets.

Caleb's eyes widened and he crossed his arms over his chest. Conquest got that Caleb didn't want to spar with the leader. Caleb had no way of knowing he would win.

"You think that is necessary?" The fake Victor pinned him with a glare.

"I do. Maybe the police turned you. Maybe you're working for them now."

The members in the room gasped and took a step back, anticipating trouble.

Victor, not as indignant as he should be, nodded. There was something "good" about him. No one else could detect it, but as a horseman, he could. Angel's work. Lightness practically dripped out of every pore, threatening to undo the evil he'd managed to accomplish before they sent him back.

"The gym would be a suitable place for said sparring. Remember, you asked for this."

Conquest glanced around the room. How did they not see he wasn't the same person? He didn't talk like that before getting arrested.

The group raced to the gym down the hall, hoots and hollers of encouragement for Victor heralding their journey.

Inside the gym, everyone took seats on the bench at the back of the room while Caleb and imposter Victor circled each other in the sparring area. Exercise equipment was out of the way against the windows. Exercise ground to a halt on the bikes when the members using them realized what was going on. They hopped down from the bikes and treadmills to join the other members on the benches.

The roar of the crowd grew louder, chants of Victor filling the room. Caleb winced, his posture changing to stooped shoulders and caved chest.

Caleb and Victor danced around each other, neither wanting to throw the first punch. As the chants in favour of Victor grew louder, Caleb's face reddened. His nostrils flared. He clenched his fists.

With a few good punches to Victor's face, Caleb smiled. He rocked his head from side to side as he darted away from the gang leader. But Victor's punch, out of nowhere, with no change in the expression on his face, sent

Caleb flying. Conquest frowned. There was angel power in that punch. He definitely couldn't leave a vessel put there by angels, in charge of the gang. They'd end up helping people, planting gardens, cleaning up the street.

Caleb shook his head and pushed himself off the floor. He charged at Victor. Ducked a few blows. Blocked a few more.

Conquest waved a hand at Caleb with as little movement as possible. He didn't want to draw attention to himself, but the man needed help. Caleb straightened as soon as the power hit him. He landed blow after blow, not letting up, no matter how much his fist might hurt.

With each blow, Victor took a step backward, wobbled, righted himself. Caleb didn't stop. He kept punching anywhere that wasn't protected. A right hook snapped Victor's head back. A punch to the gut made Victor double over. Finally, Caleb landed an uppercut that knocked Victor out.

Conquest threw a little more power, with a side of blood lust Caleb's way.

Caleb dove into Victor's body with a few more punches to the face. Then he kicked the gang leader in the stomach, the head, the legs. A man would be groaning, blocking the attack. But the vessel lay there, barely reacting until finally he stopped moving altogether.

Manny sprang off the bench. "Hold up!" He bent over Victor and touched his neck. "He's dead."

Conquest raised his hands, clapping them above his head. "That makes Caleb the new leader."

The postures of the gang members on the bench changed. They straightened their backs, then lunged off the bench to clap Caleb on the back. Pat him on the shoulder. Each vied for attention, to be recognized for congratulating him.

Caleb puffed out his chest. "Someone take care of the body. Let the other gangs know I'm in charge now."

Conquest smiled. With his job done, Conquest was leaving the gang in good hands. It took longer than he'd expected for Caleb to take over the gang, but he hadn't counted on angels sending him back to limbo.

He slipped out of the gym while the gang fawned over Caleb. It was time to get a job in the lab.

Friday evening, Becky sat on the sofa, back against the armrest facing the windows, buried in research. The sky outside was midnight dark even though it was early evening. Heavy rain pelted the windows, making satisfying plinking sounds. If she closed her eyes and listened to the rain, some of the tension in her shoulders would melt away. But she didn't have time to savour nature in action. She needed to figure out what her anonymous tipster was trying to tell her.

Leah sat at the breakfast island similarly buried, papers strewn everywhere, but with pages of information on the lost texts of the Bible. A way to defeat Death was still elusive. Since they had the information on how to send the others back, Leah was focused on the final horseman. If he arrived, the Earth was doomed, unless they found a way to stop him.

Rachel was still at work. Sarah was on her way home from the hospital, after working a little overtime.

"I found more from the lost book before Revelation, but nothing that will help. I also found mention of Armageddon in a clipping I found from the Dead Sea Scrolls."

Becky stretched her neck to loosen the muscles. "Did the clipping say anything about timing?"

"No. I'm still looking."

"I'm not having much luck with the vaccine either. I keep looking at my phone, willing the person to send me another message that will point me in the right direction."

"They will. Hey, should we start making dinner? Sarah will be home soon and Rachel should be leaving the station any minute."

Becky shook her head. "Sarah said she'd cook when she got home. If she doesn't feel like cooking, we can order in."

After over an hour in the same position on the sofa, Becky's legs cramped. Her neck hurt. Her eyes burned. If she stared at her screen much longer, a headache would form and that would make concentrating impossible.

She put her laptop on the coffee table, stood, stretched. Letting the tension melt out of her body, she held the stretch until she felt more relaxed. She walked over to the island and sat across from Leah.

"Do you need any help?"

Leah leaned forward, her eyes lit up. "I would love help."

She handed Becky a pile of papers from the lost texts she'd printed. Over the past few weeks, she'd found more photos of the texts. After weeding out the duplicates they'd already printed, she'd printed the new ones to go over whenever they had time.

"Can you read through those? I know your Enochian isn't great, but it's better than Rachel's. If you can't translate something, just ask me."

Becky nodded. Instead of returning to the sofa, she remained at the breakfast island, sitting up straight and hooking her feet on the footrest bar at the bottom of the stool. If they were here much longer, maybe they would invest in some tall chairs instead of the stools.

She read through a few of the papers, the last one causing her to go back and read it again. Waving it in the air, she caught Leah's attention.

"This one mentions signs of the apocalypse. The ground shaking, for the land will not abide being a home for destruction."

Leah frowned. "Ground shaking is an earthquake, but what does the rest mean?"

"No idea. Because why make it easy for someone to understand?"

"I'm all about the understanding at school." Leah hopped off her stool and did a few stretches. She walked over to the fridge and pulled out a pitcher of water, shaking it at Becky.

Becky nodded. "You're a teacher. You need to make it understandable to your students."

Leah poured them each a glass of water, then put the pitcher back in the fridge. "It's not easy."

Nodding, Becky took a sip of the cold water. It helped clear her mind, soothed her. Rachel didn't pick on Leah's choice of profession nearly as much as she harped on Becky's. Out of all of them, Leah's job was the least likely to help stop an apocalypse. Sure, she was good at the research and retained every single thing she read or heard, but how was that going to stop the horsemen?

Leah's eyes lit up and she plunked her glass on the breakfast bar. "I found a partial ingredient list to summon Death. I don't know if it's the same one the priest is going to use, but it looks like it should still work. I'll keep searching to confirm the same stuff is needed to send him back and see if I can find the rest of the summoning ingredients. We'll worry about getting the ingredients later."

"Good job. We'll have to confirm the priest has summoned him before we do anything." The last thing they needed was to summon the final horseman for the priest.

Half an hour later, when they were taking a break, Rachel and Sarah arrived. Sarah trudged over to the now empty sofa and crashed onto the cushions with a loud sigh.

"Long day?" Becky asked.

"The hospital just gets busier every day. And for silly things, where people should know better. Not to mention the crime-related injuries. Things are definitely getting worse out there. And I didn't even realize it until a doctor at the hospital mentioned it, but it's New Year's Eve. The ER will be bursting at the seams tonight." She pulled out a pager. "I'm on call."

Rachel eased herself onto a stool at the breakfast bar, facing the living room. "It's busy on the streets too. I'm working three homicides this week. Coincidentally, one of them is Karl Bishop, Caleb's father."

"The guy with the soul who joined the gang?" Becky sat up straighter. "You think he did it?"

Rachel narrowed her eyes. "This is not an exclusive."

"I know. I'm just curious. He has a soul. If he's killed someone else, because we know he killed someone to get into the gang, that means Conquest has him now."

Rachel craned her neck from side to side. "That's not the worst of it. The golem of Victor was found this afternoon."

"So much for bringing some light to the gang. He would have been a positive influence on them," Sarah said.

Becky's stomach grumbled. And Rachel's echoed Becky's.

Sarah groaned from the sofa and pushed herself up. "Something quick tonight okay with everyone?"

Becky got off the stool and waved her away. "You rest. Leah and I will go get burgers from the place down the street."

Sarah sighed and flopped onto the cushions again. "I'm okay with that."

Becky grabbed her purse and nodded at Leah, who grabbed her purse as well. "Same as last time?"

Rachel and Sarah nodded.

As Becky and Leah left the loft, a tingle crossed over Becky's wings. She was getting used to the power boosts. Later, she would put this into her spreadsheet and start analyzing data so she could figure out how to get all the power back.

Gunther pulled into a small-town bordering Smithville and parked his car in the parking lot of the only motel they had. He wouldn't be there long, but he hoped they had the comforts he'd come to enjoy since being summoned from limbo. Decent Wi-Fi, a firm mattress, and more than a handful of TV stations. While away from the city, he needed to stay connected to the rest of the world, monitor the news, adjust plans if needed.

Despite having only one motel, the town, a village really, boasted ten restaurants or pubs. In all of those, there had to be a decent burger.

He checked into the motel, took his key, an actual key, not a key card like most hotels used, and found his room on the first floor. Based on the emptiness of the parking lot, he guessed he was the only guest in the place. Wavecrest was the town you passed through to get to other more exciting places. A dwindling population due to lack of jobs would someday see the hamlet vanish, absorbed into neighbouring Smithville or Grassie.

He dropped his bag on the bed, did a quick perusal of the room, then left. Later, after he'd confirmed the project was on target, he would return to the room to explore the few amenities they had.

Leaving the car in the lot, he walked the short distance to the edge of town where a tall metal fence blocked off a large patch of land. Inside the fence, a small building looked lonely and out of place among the construction vehicles. The foreman of the project would spend a lot of time there.

He flicked his hand where the two sides of the gate came together, secured shut with a thick metal chain and padlock. The lock clicked open and he removed the chain, pushing the gate wide enough so he could slip through.

A sharp knock on the door brought a crashing sound from inside the building. A curse followed, then pounding footsteps. The foreman, James, swung the door open, his eyes widening when he saw Gunther. Wearing new jeans, a denim dress shirt with more wrinkles than a Shar Pei, and hair spiking in all directions, the man appeared to have been sleeping.

"I wasn't expecting you until Monday."

Gunther pushed past him, noting the sofa on the left side of the room with a blanket strewn across the cushions. On the right was a small metal desk, a filing cabinet, and a drafting board for creating the plans. In the middle, against the wall, was a small table with a few mugs, a coffee maker, and a sugar bowl. Beside the table was a small fridge.

"I have to be in Alberta on Monday. I wanted to make sure everything here was going as planned."

James gestured to the chairs in front of the desk. "Yes. As long as the temperature doesn't dip, we're breaking ground on Monday." He sat behind the desk. "It will take some time to get to the depth and width specified in the plans. Then pouring the foundation for it. But I'm confident we'll be able to finish it on time."

Gunther smiled, taking a seat in one of the chairs across from him. "There's a bonus in it for you the faster you can get it built."

He didn't tell the foreman about the weapons he needed to move from Alberta before the inspection. If it was possible to get them relocated by then, it would make his life easier. If not, Death's reaper would have to figure out something. It's not like they hadn't been covering up this stuff for years already. But now that they were so close, he couldn't risk one of the other people on the inspection committee suspecting anything. Internet rumours were already running rampant that the Canadian government was hiding something.

"I've been working around the clock to make sure everything is in place. All the permits are up to date. I've had the crew testing the ground to make sure it's not too cold. We've had an unseasonably warm winter so far. If that keeps up, the bunker will be operational in no time."

With the weapons here, it would make fitting the warheads easier. If he couldn't move them soon, the plan was still a go. It would just be a little more difficult, requiring more reaper intervention than he'd like. Death was the most impartial of all the horsemen and wouldn't be coaxed to kill people who weren't on his list. People had to get on Death's list on their own. And sometimes that meant one of the other horsemen had to be the bad guy. A lot of people would end up on Death's list when Gunther was finished with his weapons.

"Good. Keep me apprised."

Gunther left the small building, locked the gate, and

stalked back to the motel. He would stay in town for the weekend in case any issues popped up. He hoped everything went like clockwork. It would be nice for an apocalypse to go off without a hitch for a change. Not like the last few times he'd been on Earth. The promise of war had been intoxicating, but ultimately small squabbles between neighbouring countries weren't enough and he'd gone back to limbo.

This time there could be nothing left to chance. War was on the horizon. He just needed to push it along.

Chapter Six

Late Saturday afternoon, the sun sank in the sky. Light blue skies were accented with soft puffs of white clouds. Becky watched from the sofa as a blue jay flew by as it veered up and away from the window. Probably to the rooftop garden they'd neglected since Leah arrived. There wasn't much they could do with it in winter, but some of the small evergreens might need to be tended to.

As it was most weekends, Sarah and Rachel were at work, despite not being scheduled to be there. Since her normal shifts at the hospital kept her busy, Sarah went in on weekends to check on patients and do follow-up tests. Rachel tended to use the weekends to catch up on paperwork and make calls she couldn't get to during the week. The two of them worked too hard. Half the time, Becky thought Rachel worked on weekends to get away from her. The oldest angel liked the other two well enough, but for some reason, she and Rachel grated on each other's nerves.

Leah sat on the chair in the living room, laptop open. Becky assumed the youngest angel was searching for ancient texts still. It seemed that was all she did when she wasn't at the school teaching. Dishes from their lunch still littered the coffee table. They'd have to tidy up before Sarah got home or endure her lecture about cleanliness for the hundredth time.

Becky scrolled through emails and social media, taking a short break from the research into the flu vaccine. Interns were expertly handling other research for her so she would be able to sound knowledgeable when doing her stories next week. Frankly, the tipster and the flu texts were giving her a headache. She didn't like it, at all. An angel shouldn't have to deal with pain.

Her phone, beside her on the sofa, buzzed. She snatched it up to see a message fading from the screen. She swiped to open it and frowned at the red dot on her text messages app. She clicked the icon to pull up the message, knowing it would be another cryptic tip that led her nowhere.

> What about the weapons?

> X

She was beginning to think she was being pranked by someone at the TV station, but even though she got along with everyone there, none were close enough to prank her. If they weren't fighting to stop an apocalypse, would she have made friends at work? It didn't bother her that she only went out with her sisters, but if things were different, maybe she'd want a life outside of family and work.

What weapons? The tipster hadn't mentioned weapons before. What kind? Did the flu vaccine have something to do with weapons now? What was she supposed to look for this time in her research?

She sat up straighter on the sofa. Was someone

weaponizing something? Her heart raced, and a rush of adrenaline at the prospect of a breaking story energized her. If that was the end game of all these messages she'd been receiving, who was the weapon going to be used on? Too many questions ricocheted through her mind. She needed to focus on one of them and see if it led anywhere.

She opened a new tab and put weapons in the search engine. Too many pages to sift through came back. If the tipster had been more specific with the kind of weapons, that might have helped. A term as vague as weapons could mean anything. Street weapons? Rachel would be more help with that sort of information.

Frustrated, she clicked the search engine's icon to bring her back to a blank search page. She tapped her fingers on the keyboard, thinking about what to search for this time.

Her phone buzzed again. Another text flashed across the screen. One word.

Ralston

X

She typed the word into the search engine and hit enter. She fist-bumped the air even though there were over three million results. The first one on the page, about a village called Ralston in Alberta, looked promising. She clicked on the link and quickly scanned the article. Pretty much the only thing there was a Canadian Forces Base. She clicked on the link to CFB Ralston. The beginning of that article touted the base as the second largest in the country, used for chemical and biological warfare training.

Becky's heart raced. Possibilities ran through her mind, less generalized, more focused, but all bombarding her brain at the same time. Though she couldn't piece everything together yet, the strands were there. If she picked up the right string, she knew she could make sense of everything.

The page was replete with links to articles about the agencies mentioned in the piece. Before she clicked on anything, she read the whole article and bookmarked it. Then she clicked on one of the first links to an article about CDRD Ralston. According to the article, Canadian Defence Research and Development Ralston, renamed Defence Research Ralston, was the research facility, one of eight centres making up the CDRD. The article explained that Canadian Defence Research and Development was part of the Canadian Department of Defence that dealt with the scientific and technological needs of the Canadian forces. Besides weapons systems evaluation and military engineering, the site also dealt with chemical and biological defence.

With so many links in the article, she didn't know which one to click next. Which one would give her another rabbit hole to disappear into? While she didn't need to know all the inner workings of the military facilities, she did need to know about weapons. Since the first few text messages were about the flu vaccine, she clicked a link for the Biological and Chemical Defence Audit Committee.

"What's going on? Why the frown?"

Leah's question startled Becky. She shook her head and pointed to the computer screen. "So much information. Did you know there's a committee that oversees all the military bases to make sure they aren't stockpiling weapons? And that they only have enough biological agents to perform testing and to help with defence?"

Lowering the lid of her laptop, Leah smiled. "Got a tip you could actually use this time?"

Becky nodded. "And how. The links in these articles alone are going to send me down a rabbit hole of research for days. I found the committee's website and I'm going to read some of the reports. Hopefully, I'll be able to understand them. I still don't know what it all means yet, but I have a direction now."

Leah put her laptop on the coffee table and stood, stretching her limbs like she was a dancer preparing to go on stage. "I need a break. You want anything from the kitchen?"

"No, thanks. I'll get something later. Right now, it might distract me from something important." Becky clicked on the link to the first report. "Whoa."

Leah rushed back to the living room. "What?"

Becky turned her laptop so Leah could read the screen. The cover page of the report took up the entire screen. "The microbiologist Dr. Karimi told us about, Dr. Althaus, is on the committee."

"So things are coming together." Leah padded back to the kitchen.

"Yes. It's going to take some time to digest all of this. And figure out how any of this has anything to do with this year's flu vaccine."

"Good question." Leah returned to her chair with a bowl of ice cream. She pulled her computer back onto her lap and began typing again.

Becky's head started to pound. She pushed her computer away and focused on Leah. "What are you working on?"

Leah looked up with the spoon still in her mouth. She pulled the cutlery out with a clink against her teeth. "Planning a day trip for my grade twelve history class to the ROM. There are some exhibits there on loan from the Vatican that I want to look at."

"I didn't know the Royal Ontario Museum did field

trips. Rachel will be happy about that. We need more information on the lost texts."

"I'm not sure that's what they are, but it can't hurt to look."

"Well, it's better than what I've got, which is more questions. Tips about weapons and a flu vaccine. Are there more viruses being held than there should be? The report from last year checks out. I'm going to see if I can contact someone on Monday."

"If you want me to help with anything, let me know."

Becky put her laptop on the coffee table and stood. "I'll let you know. I'm going to start making dinner. Sarah and Rachel should be home soon. We can have an early dinner, then maybe go to the bar for a few drinks."

An hour later, instead of sitting around the island eating a home-cooked meal, they sat at their usual table at the back of Baron's, waiting for a waitress to bring them their food. Becky's attempt at cooking had been a disaster, her mind still trying to make sense of all the data she'd seen after the last text her tipster had sent. Sarah, not happy with the state of the kitchen, had immediately attempted to clean so she could make dinner. When Becky had suggested the bar, everyone had agreed.

Their drinks, already sitting in front of them, provided a small distraction while they waited. A waitress bustled over and deposited a basket of bread in the middle of the table, with a small metal bowl of whipped butter. Becky's stomach grumbled.

"Anyone want me to cut them a slice?"

Rachel and Leah shook their heads. Sarah nodded.

Even though she'd burnt the pasta, making food had

kicked her hunger into overdrive. Becky cut a thick slice of the crusty bread for herself and one for Sarah. Slathering it with a thick coat of butter, her mouth watered.

She took a bite and savoured the creaminess of the butter and the slightly nutty flavour of the bread. If dinner took much longer, she would fill up on carbs.

Rachel took a sip of her drink. "There are no leads on Karl Bishop's death. More distressing is the news that Caleb is the leader of the Grange gang now, according to Detective Littman."

Becky finished chewing and swallowed before she choked. "Wow. Quite the fall for him. Conquest was able to get a souled person to choose evil."

Sarah put her bread down on the small plate beside her cutlery. "Conquest will be more powerful now. With more influence. He'll be able to turn others with souls faster."

"Definitely not good news," Rachel said.

Becky's phone, face up on the table, buzzed. Ellen's name flashed on the screen. "It's my producer. I have to take this."

She grabbed the phone, swiping to answer the call as she stood. "Becky Malak."

Ellen's sigh of relief sent Becky's disaster instincts into overdrive.

"Becky, the peace talks are being moved to Ottawa."

"What happened?"

Becky took the opportunity presented by the call to walk around the bar to do a soul count. So far no one had one.

"The talks in Prague broke down after the four-day break. Both parties wanted a change of scenery. They agreed to keep talking if the talks were moved somewhere else. They start next Monday. I expect you to be in Ottawa on Friday."

"Friday. That's not a lot of notice." Five days' notice was plenty, but she didn't want Ellen to think she was always available. She'd be bringing her laptop anyway. As long as she had an internet connection, she could do research anywhere. Her tipster would still be able to text her.

"I know. Sorry about that. I'm sending you an eticket. Henry will be going with you."

Henry would be even less pleased than she was to be flying to Ottawa on short notice. He had a life outside work, with a girlfriend and friends who wanted to spend time with him. She finished the call, continued with her circuit of the floor, then made her way back to the table. Their meals had arrived and she dug into her fries before she sat back down.

"No souls in the audience tonight."

"Is there a way to tell how many were in purgatory before Death killed off most of them?" Rachel asked.

"I can't find a time in history except for the Black Death when the death rate was greater than the birth rate," Leah said.

Rachel frowned. "Great. So more and more people without souls are being born. Will it take something as bad as the Black Death before people are born with souls again?"

Leah nodded. "Yes. Assuming some of the people who die have souls. And some of those still have something to accomplish on Earth and go to purgatory instead of Heaven."

Rachel's frown deepened. "We need a miracle."

Sarah reached out and snagged a few French fries from Rachel's plate. "We're angels. That's what we do. We'll help everyone here. You'll see. That's why I put in so many hours at the hospital."

Rachel batted Sarah's hand away when the doctor tried to steal more fries. "Speaking of Death. If he's always here, how do we get rid of him?"

Leah sat up straighter, eyes wide, and shook her head. "The incarnation from Revelation isn't always here. But his reapers are. The one from Revelation is all his reapers and him combined into one being."

Becky put her burger down to focus on Leah. "When the priest calls him, all the reapers will join together?"

Leah nodded. "No reapers, no one going to Heaven or purgatory. Souls just hanging around on Earth."

Sarah shuddered. "And Death so powerful he can wipe out swaths of people with a single wave of his hand. If War is here, so many people will be on Death's list."

"With his job done, Death will release the reapers again to gather any souls that might have been here." Leah took a sip of her drink.

Rachel clapped her hands to get their attention. "Let's deal with one of them at a time. Focus on War. If we can send him back, we can at least slow Father Ianetti down while we figure out our next moves."

Becky scarfed down her hamburger and shoved the rest of her fries away. Sarah piled them all onto her own plate. With less than a week until she had to be in Ottawa, Becky needed to get a few things done before leaving for the airport. She'd have to delegate more research to Laura and the other interns. At least she might be able to figure something out while at the peace summit. With the talks being moved to the capital, maybe War would pay a visit. It was hard to fight someone they hadn't met and didn't know what they looked like.

Chapter Seven

Monday, a few hours before Becky had to be on camera for the evening news, she sat in her office at the TV station, going through past reports of the audit committee. All of them were basically the same, telling her the same things. There were no stock piles of weapons or viral agents at any of the bases across Canada. The reports indicated everyone cooperated fully, gave the team access to their labs and testing facilities and a tour of the base.

She'd been in research mode all weekend. So much information was stuffed into her brain, she couldn't make sense of it all. Those strings were still dangling and she wasn't able to tie them all together. Yet.

The microbiologist that Dr. Karimi told her about was on the committee. The woman had emailed him with answers to the questions Becky had about the vaccine, but that didn't mean Becky couldn't march down to wherever the woman had an office and talk to her. In her investigation into the microbiologist, Becky learned she taught at the university nearby.

Becky picked up the receiver on her phone and called

Laura's extension. Her intern picked it up immediately. "What's up?"

"Laura, could you find me the office on campus for Dr. Isolde Althaus?"

"Right away." Laura hung up, leaving Becky listening to a dial tone.

Becky replaced the receiver in its cradle and shuffled through some of the papers on her desk. If she were more organized, she'd probably do her research a lot more efficiently. But she knew where everything was in her multiple piles. Once in a while, she would straighten them to make the desk look tidier, but she never put them away while she was working on a story.

Right now she was working on a few. Ellen wanted her to do some background work for the peace talks that were being moved. She also had the follow-up to the gang violence piece that needed more research. And the thing with the vaccine and the weapons.

She hoped Dr. Althaus would be able to help her with the last story.

Laura buzzed her again. Becky picked up the phone and jotted down the information she gave her.

"Do you want me to go? You could give me a list of questions to ask." Laura always wanted to be helpful.

"No, I'll go. I need to do this. Would you be able to help the other interns with their research in the meantime?"

"No problem."

Becky thanked her and hung up. The office was in the Faculty of Science building at the university.

Becky hit the home button on her phone to check the time. She had at least two hours before she needed to be back to go on the air.

She opened her bottom drawer and retrieved her

purse. A familiar tingle flowed over her wings. Knowing what it meant, she vowed to check it later. And add the incident to her growing list of data.

She calculated what would be faster. Walking to the university or taking the subway. The subway won, due mostly to the fact she didn't want to rush. Undue exertion would cause her to perspire and she didn't have time to take a shower again.

After some trial and error, she found the Faculty of Science building. A modern-looking structure with sleek lines and high windows, sterile was the first word that popped into her head. She walked up the stairs, through the doors, and searched for signs indicating offices for faculty.

Spotting a sign that indicated the microbiology department was to the right, Becky hurried down the hallway, checking room numbers as she went. Out of breath, she stopped at the end of the corridor and knocked on the door on the left.

A quiet, yet firm voice told her to enter. Becky pushed the door open and smiled at the petite, auburn-haired woman who sat behind a desk so big it made her look like a doll. An adjustable chair brought the woman up to a spot so she could see over the top of the desk. Folders, piled high on each side, looked like columns, ready to support a ceiling above them.

The woman smelled different. Perhaps it was from the chemicals in the lab or a special brand of soap, or strong sanitizer. But she didn't smell like any of the souled or soulless Becky had encountered so far. That was a mystery to solve another day if time permitted.

"Dr. Althaus, I'm Becky Malak. Dr. Karimi sent you questions for me."

The doctor looked up, gave her a distracted smile, and

her tongue jutted out for a split second. "Yes, there's nothing wrong with the vaccine."

"May I?" Becky gestured to a chair in front of the desk, also covered in folders. When the woman nodded, Becky lifted the documents and put them gently on the floor.

"That's not why I came." Becky sat, resting her hands on her knees. "I want to know about the visits to the bases for the weapons and biological agents checks."

Dr. Althaus leaned back in her chair. "What more can I tell you? It's all in the report. I'm assuming you read the report?"

"Yes. But when are you doing another inspection?"

The woman moved her mouse and clicked on something. "In a few weeks. It's always the same. Always compliant."

Becky stood. "Thanks for your time."

She hurried out of the room, down the hall, and out of the building. Why didn't she believe the scientist? The hair on the back of her neck rose, and goose bumps erupted on her arms. There was something the doctor was keeping from her, but she didn't have time to grill her. She had enough time to get back to the station and to the makeup chair before going on-air.

***

Gunther slowed the rental car as he approached the turnoff for the Canadian Forces Base Ralston. He turned onto the street, stopped at the security booth, and presented his credentials to the guard on duty. The man saluted, raised the gate, and waved him through. Gunther smiled. He liked the respect of being a high-ranking military man.

He passed an old tank that sat on the grass at one of

the crossroads. Ignoring the nostalgia of checking out the vehicle, he continued along the road until he arrived at the office building. Located at the end of the main road, the building was a squat three storeys of red brick. A main door in the front, with security, was the only official method of ingress and egress, though there were two emergency exits at either side of the building.

He parked in the lot on the right side of the building and marched to the main entryway. There was no reason his ID shouldn't work, but he still held his breath as the security guard swiped the card. A soft beep, and a green light on the security display gave him access. The turnstile clicked, unlocking it, and Gunther pushed through the gate. The guard handed back his card.

He walked down the hall, nodding at people with memories of him in the job for years. He gracefully ducked away from friendly invitations to reminisce about old times, blaming work for the reason he had to go. It was an unfortunate side effect of creating this persona. One with a long and decorated military background would have friends and colleagues eager to catch up when he was in town. That's why he had to make the trip short.

At the end of the hall, there was a double set of doors on the right that led into another part of the building. Only top-level clearance was permitted through the doors. Immediately after passing through there was a wide concrete staircase. He ran down the stairs to a landing that had a single elevator. He pressed the call button, his fingerprint providing the credentials to show he had the security clearance to ride the elevator.

When the cab arrived, he entered the small car, pressed the only button there was for a floor, and waited for the doors to close. The car lurched as it began its descent to lower levels of the complex that only high-ranking officials knew about.

The car opened on sub level twelve. Dark grey walls absorbed much of the light flickering from the overhead fluorescent bulbs. This far underground, he expected the air to smell dank and musty, but the thick, reinforced concrete walls absorbed not only sound, but prevented the smells of the surrounding earth from creeping in.

Housed on this level were the weapons he needed to move and the lab where the defence aspect of viruses was tested. Once tested and defence applications established, the viruses were destroyed, at least on paper. But they sent vials of what the apocalypse movement deemed agent Omega to a lab in Ontario that was manufacturing far more of the virus than they needed to test with. It would be less dangerous to the plan to bring the weapons to Ontario and to the biological agent than it would be to bring the quantity of the agent he needed here.

He headed for the weapons bunker at the far end of the corridor. Again, he used his fingerprint to gain access. Once inside, he pulled out the paperwork for decommissioning the weapons from a filing cabinet against the wall, sat at the small metal desk set to the right, and ticked all the boxes, dotted all the Is, crossed all the Ts. To decommission them, they would be sent to a base in Ontario, the new location he was having built in Fort Erie. Of course there was no actual military base there at the address he was sending the weapons to, but no one in the military would know that. He'd painted a huge picture when he created his persona.

Paperwork in hand, he left the bunker, returned to the office level of the building, and dropped the pile of papers off at a supervisor's desk to travel up the chain the rest of the way. With a little magic attached to the paperwork, it would bypass red tape and get approved in a timely manner. Moving the weapons closer to a U.S. border would get his plan in motion. The decommissioning part would take place at the new bunker and of course wouldn't happen. He needed them to be operational, but he needed the paperwork to look like everything was above board in case there was scrutiny. And now that he knew there were angels in the mix, he needed to make sure they weren't able to deduce his plan.

He put in some time in his office for appearances' sake. With his door open so anyone walking by would know he was there. Once he was satisfied he'd done all he could do there, he locked up his office, said goodbye to the officer who would be signing off on the paperwork, then left the base.

He needed to be in Ontario for the eventual hand-off of the weapons and that was where most of the action was going to happen when the plan went into effect. He wanted to be ready for the show.

Becky gave a subdued smile to the camera, then a slight nod. "And that's the news at six. Kevin Moore will have your news at eleven."

She unclipped her microphone when the red record light winked out on top of the camera. With all the chaos going on around them, she needed something calming. Thankfully, Rachel had agreed that too much work would burn them out, so tonight was all about unwinding, relaxing, and general chat at Baron's. No apocalypse talk if possible, just sisters enjoying each other's company.

She raced back to her office to grab her purse. Her stomach grumbled. Thankful it had waited until after the broadcast to announce its lack of food, she put on her coat and slung her purse over her shoulder.

In the elevator, she pulled out her phone and called Sarah's number. She was probably still at the hospital, helping out in the ER after her official shift ended. A moment later, Steve's familiar playlist from the bar filtered through the phone.

"You left work on time." Surprise filled her voice.

"Nope. I needed a day off, for real this time. It was glorious. And I got some angel power back."

"Tell me all the details later so I can put it in the spreadsheet. Right now, though, I'm calling to find out if we need anything at home."

Sarah rattled off a list of items they were running low on, the most important of which was ice cream.

"I'll stop to pick them up on my way to the bar. I'll be late, so order me a cheeseburger and fries."

After she ended the call, a tingle went across her wings. She was beginning to love that feeling. But she wished she could get her wings back to full power in one fell swoop of a tingle.

Fifteen minutes later, she walked into the market where Felicia Newman was murdered a few weeks ago. It looked like nothing had happened there. All the shelves were stocked, no blood marred the floor, and even the stains were gone. Whoever the shopkeeper had hired for cleanup had done an excellent job. The only sign that something awful had happened was the protective partition that separated the cashier from the customer at the check-out counter. By the looks of it, bulletproof.

Except Felicia hadn't been working there when she was killed. She'd been a customer. The partition wouldn't help them if the gangs decided to do another initiation.

She shoved the thoughts from her mind. Tonight was

supposed to be about relaxing, getting out of their own heads for a bit.

She rushed down the aisles, picking up everything Sarah had mentioned, paid for it, then left the shop. Evening rush hour had died down a bit, enabling her to navigate the sidewalks without having to dodge a lot of people on her way back to the loft.

Inside, she put all the groceries and sundry items away. Standing in the middle of the kitchen, she marvelled at how quiet the place was. The hum of the refrigerator was the only noise in the place. It was nice having the loft to herself even for a few moments. Since falling from Heaven, she was always around someone. Either one or all of her sisters were with her at the loft. Or she was at work, surrounded by colleagues, interviewing people. Even when she was in her office following up on research, Kevin Moore was usually there with her.

Her stomach grumbled again, reminding her she had a cheeseburger waiting for her at Baron's.

She left the loft and hurried to the bar. At the back in their usual spots, Rachel, Sarah, and Leah were already eating their meals. She took her seat and popped a fry into her mouth. Above the bar, the big screen TV was tuned to the local twenty-four-hour news channel. Headlines scrolled along the bottom of the screen while the left side featured story segments and live news footage. And the right side updated viewers on the weather and commute times.

"I was starving. So glad this was already here."

"Lucky you got here when you did," Rachel said. "Sarah was about to eat your cheeseburger."

"I was not."

Becky looked at Sarah's plate and noted the pile of fries beside her pasta. "Really? So just the fries then?"

Sarah blushed. "They're good fries."

Becky took a large bite of her cheeseburger. If they'd had these when she was alive, she would have devoured one every night. From her cloud in Heaven, looking down on all those people, she'd watched humans eat burgers, not knowing what she was missing. In Heaven, they didn't need to eat unless they wanted to, and even then it wasn't real food, just simulations that didn't give you the exact flavors as the real thing.

The news scroll on the TV had switched to the peace talks being moved to Ottawa. She frowned. Unless they pulled off a miracle by Monday, she knew how the talks were going to go. Downhill faster than a gold medal skier.

Above the scroll about the talks was a shot of the doomsday clock. It ticked one minute closer to midnight.

Chapter Eight

Walking down an aisle of cubicles with Laura Tuesday afternoon after lunch, Becky smiled and nodded to her co-workers. No one took the same lunch. The workload was always heavy, and you squeezed in a few minutes when you could. Today, she'd needed more time away from her desk than a quick bathroom break, so she and Laura had gone down to the cafeteria.

Becky held a small salad in her hand for later, if she got the munchies. She didn't want to have to make another trip down, and the cafeteria closed for most items at two o'clock.

"My fiancé says we should go to Paris for our honeymoon," Laura said.

Becky's heart kicked up a notch. She hoped there would be a wedding. That the earth was still chugging along by then with most of its humans still around to enjoy the ride. She didn't want to tell Laura to move up the wedding day. What would she say? So, there's going to be an apocalypse. Any chance you can get married now?

At Laura's cubicle, they paused. Laura pulled out her

chair, tossed the snack-sized bag of chips she'd brought with her from the cafeteria onto her keyboard, and smiled. Becky noted the pictures of Laura and her fiancé on the desk. Pictures of Laura and friends. Still more pictures of Laura with some of the other interns from the station. Beside her computer, there was a small plant, thriving even though it was cooped up indoors in a small pot. Post-it notes for little messages to herself adorned the wall of the cubicle where her computer sat.

"Thanks for the chat," Becky said.

"Anytime. It was nice to get away for a bit. Even if it was only half an hour."

Half an hour. Seemed like five minutes.

Becky trudged to her office. Looking at it from a subjective perspective, it could be anyone's office. On her side, almost no personalization gave any clues as to who occupied the space. Only one picture sat on the desk of her and the other angels. Leah was added later, once she arrived and worked her magic to create a life for herself.

Kevin's desk, flush against the wall at the entrance to the room, held pictures of him and his wife, their kids, his boat. Some knick-knacks he'd brought back from his travels as a reporter.

Becky sat at her desk, empty of memories, full of work. She spent so much time here, but she couldn't afford to think of it like a job the way everyone else did. This was a mission. She couldn't be distracted with frivolous stuff.

She pushed the lone picture aside, so it was on the very corner of the desk. She unlocked her computer and pulled up her email inbox. How many messages had she missed by going downstairs for a change?

At least a dozen new emails had come in while she was gone. Before she could click on the bottom one, her phone buzzed. She pulled it out of her pants pocket, hoping this time, if it was another tip, her tipster gave her something to work with.

A text message filled the screen.

> Put the pieces together.
>
> X

They sounded like they were getting annoyed. She gave a low chuckle. *Join the club, pal.* Put the pieces together how? If everything passed inspection, why was she getting these tips? Nothing seemed out of the ordinary, so what was she supposed to look for?

Teeth clenched, she blew out a breath and fired off a text to the person.

> What exactly should I be looking for?
>
> B

A few seconds later, another text popped up. She let out another breath, then unclenched her jaw when her head started to throb. She couldn't believe they texted back. She was sure that after each message, the person tossed the phone and got another burner phone.

> You will learn.
>
> X

Becky frowned. The vagueness of the response annoyed her. Learn what? Maybe they had to be cryptic in case someone got a hold of the phone. She yanked the receiver off her phone and punched in Laura's extension, asking the intern to come to her office when she answered.

Seconds later, Laura stood in the doorway. "Reporting for duty." She flashed a smile.

"Good. I need help."

Laura plopped down into the chair opposite Becky. "What's up?"

Becky handed her the cell phone with the messages up on the screen. "Learn what?"

Laura leaned back in the chair, touched a fingertip to her lips, and narrowed her eyes. "Good question. Where do you learn?"

"School. But they can't mean Leah's school. Could they?"

"Maybe. She teaches history, right?"

"Yes. Learn from history. You also learn in university."

Laura's eyes lit up. "That has to be it. The university."

Becky pulled up her notes about the university. "It specializes in medicine and employs Dr. Isolde Althaus, who is on the Biological and Chemical Defence Audit Committee."

"The crumbs are leading to her or at least the committee," Laura said.

Becky nodded, convinced it was more than that. It wasn't just the tips leading her to the university, it was that plus the tips on weapons that had her skin crawling.

"I need to go there to talk to her. Maybe she'll be more willing to talk at the lab instead of her office at the university. Want to come?"

"Love to."

"Great. Get your purse. We're leaving in five minutes."

Inside the building that housed Queen City University Research Group, adjacent to the university, Becky and Laura waited for someone to arrive to show them the facility. The entryway of the building was small, with only one chair for visitors, a desk with a receptionist behind it, and a partition blocking off the back of the room from the entryway. After asking what their business was and then calling for the director of the lab, Dr. Sean Gardner, the receptionist was back to reading through an old magazine.

Ten minutes after their arrival, a tall man with broad shoulders and muscled arms who looked like he spent more time at a gym than a lab, wearing a white lab coat, came through a steel door and smiled at them. The smile didn't reach the man's brown eyes.

"How can I help you?"

He reached out a hand to shake theirs. After quick introductions, Becky smiled. "We were hoping to talk to Dr. Althaus. She does work here?"

"Yes, she does. I'm afraid she's very busy in the lab right now."

Not wanting to resort to magic, Becky frowned. "We won't take long. She talked to me in her office in the Faculty of Science building yesterday. I had some follow-up."

He shook his head. "I can answer anything you want to know."

With a sigh, Becky touched his arm again, giving him magical authorization. She peeked over her shoulder to make sure Laura hadn't seen anything. If the magic was focused, small, the energy was barely noticeable, but her intern was perceptive.

Laura clasped her purse as if ready to leave.

"I guess it wouldn't hurt for you to speak to her." He nodded at the receptionist and she handed over guest security cards with clips.

He handed them to Becky and Laura, who clipped them onto the belt loops of their slacks.

"You'll have to go through the protocols, of course. And Dr. Althaus will come out of the inner lab to you."

"We expected that. What BSL is the lab?"

"It's a two. We deal with potentially lethal contagions, the flu, yellow fever, West Nile virus."

He punched in a code on a panel beside the steel door. The panel beeped, then the door whooshed open. Inside, there was a door to the left that led to the office area. Ahead of them was a corridor that came to an end at an elevator at the back wall.

If she was remembering her research correctly, it looked like BSL 4 protocols were in place.

On the floor with the lab, Becky and Laura waited for Dr. Gardner to get Dr. Althaus.

"I didn't think they'd let us down here." Laura kept a keen eye on the huge glass wall separating them from the corridor to the actual labs.

"Me neither. I'm glad they did, though."

She would know soon if her use of power did them any good. Standing out here wasn't going to tell them much. She wanted to see the lab properly, even if she couldn't stand inside it. Right now they were still too far away from where anything happened.

Finally, Dr. Gardner hurried down the corridor. He opened the door for them and gestured down the hallway. "There are some safety protocols to get into the lab. We have two labs and a research area."

Heart pounding, Becky followed the director, Laura beside her, to a metal door. Once there, they went through the typical BSL 2 protocols for entering, then passed through another metal door to the research area, but the people inside the lab on the left wore positive pressure suits. And on the right was the lab with BSL 2 protocols.

Inside the research area of the lab, still separated from

the lab itself, she turned to the director. "You say this has a BSL of two, is that correct?"

He nodded. "For some time now."

She watched his face for signs of deception. Either he truly believed the lab was biosafety level two, or he was a very good liar.

In the lab on the right, two people, a man and a woman, in lab coats talked at a station at the back of the room. When the woman looked up, the director motioned for her to come over. The man she'd been talking to also looked up. A sudden wave of dizziness swept over Becky and she took a step back, sucking in a deep breath. Conquest, looking like a scientist, glanced over, then went back to whatever he'd been doing with the petri dishes.

Once through the door from the lab to the research area, Dr. Althaus stalked over, her lips thinned to almost non-existence. "How can I help you?"

"You do lab work and teach?"

"Yes. I only teach one class and the lab is almost right on campus, so it works out. Is this about the vaccine again? We're working on another one that is more effective."

Beside Becky, Laura had pulled out a notepad and pen to take notes.

"That is good to know."

"Did you want to see the data for the new vaccine?" Dr. Althaus tapped on the glass wall separating the research room from the lab. "Vic."

Conquest looked over at them.

Did he recognize her? With Conquest here, at the lab, the tips had to be connected to the apocalypse. But how was that possible? Unless the actions the tipster was warning her about would help further the end of the world.

Her head spinning, she hastily shook the director's

hand. "Thank you so much for giving us the brief tour. We must be going now."

She grabbed Laura's arm and dragged her back to the metal door. Once outside the protocol area, they sanitized their hands with the gel provided.

Outside, Becky took a deep breath to calm her racing heart.

"What's going on?"

Becky wished she could tell Laura more. Conquest being there confirmed this new vaccine wouldn't be what it said on the label either.

"I didn't want to tip my hand how suspicious I am of them. Something is going on at that lab. Let's get back to the station."

Back in her office, door closed, Becky pulled out her phone and sent a group text to the other angels, letting them know about Conquest. He was done with the gangs, and now he was messing with medicine. A chill slithered down Becky's back.

After her broadcast, Becky sat at her desk, going through all the notes she'd compiled about the vaccine, weapons, the CFB in Ralston, plus the text messages from her tipster. Everything was printed and in piles on her desk to make it easy to shuffle through. Having it all printed took away the ability to do a text search, but sometimes she needed to have paper in hand when she was researching a story. The ability to highlight and shuffle things around helped her form cohesive ideas. She needed that right now, because nothing was making sense to her. What did vaccines have to do with weapons?

She pulled out the reports from the committee. If the

bases passed inspection every year, why was her tipster sending her tips? She didn't quite believe what Dr. Althaus said about the new vaccine. Or the old one for that matter.

She picked up her phone and called Laura's extension. Since it was after the supper time broadcast, all the interns might be gone, but usually a few lingered. The late-night news still needed research.

Laura picked up the phone. "Need help with something?"

Letting out a sigh of relief, Becky wound the cord around her finger. "Yes. I need any research you can get me on the committee that goes to the bases to check on the status of their weapons. Especially Dr. Althaus. Anything you can find."

"You got it."

While she waited for Laura's exceptional research skills to provide fruit, Becky pulled up the lab's website. She clicked the about tab to find out more background on the facility. They listed the vaccines they'd been responsible for and what upcoming vaccines they had a hand in. Most of the vaccines were for the flu and every year they were successful. So why was it not as effective this year?

This was the year the apocalypse had been fast-tracked. But did anyone but the priest know that was going to happen? How much reach did the priest's connections go? How many members of the Omega sect were helping him instead of being bystanders? He obviously wasn't doing it alone since he had to summon the horsemen. But what else had he done?

An email popped into her inbox with the subject line "Apocalypse sermons."

She clicked on the message and scanned it. Her stomach roiled. Churches around the world were now doing apocalypse sermons based on Father Ianetti's predictions of the impending apocalypse.

Great.

That was all they needed. It was bad enough that one priest was predicting the end of the world, but now others were jumping on the arc. If the others were also involved in actions that would help the apocalypse along or belonged to the Omega sect, they had even more work cut out for them.

She had to trust that Father Ianetti was the ring master, the one holding all the cards for bringing about the end. They needed to stop him and the horsemen to turn things around before the destruction got too far.

Laura swept into Becky's office less than an hour later, arms laden with papers.

Grateful for the interruption and the halting of where her mind was headed, she smiled. "That was fast. What did you find?"

Laura spread out photos on top of Becky's desk. "These are photos of the committee going back to its inception in 1990. In all of them, one person is always a slight blur."

She pointed to the person in each photo. Under the photo, different names appeared for each blur, except for the most recent committee members, who had been doing the job for three years.

They might be a blur for Laura, but for Becky, they were crystal clear. All the blurs were Dr. Isolde Althaus.

Different names, same person. How many more pictures of them would she find if she searched? In every photo, they looked exactly the same age. Nothing about them had changed, with the exception of hairstyle and clothes to match the time period.

Close to weapons and viral agents. The first thing that

popped into her head was reaper. She knew they were always on earth. They had a job to do and weren't good or evil. They just were. But with the right incentive, the proper persuasion, they could be swayed to help evil. And that's what the priest was, at least to her. Evil.

"This is great, Laura. You should get home to your fiancé. I'll be leaving soon too."

Laura dipped her head. "Thanks. See you tomorrow."

Once Laura was gone, Becky pulled out her phone to send another group text. With a reaper in charge of the new vaccine, things were going to get worse.

Chapter Nine

Wednesday morning, Gunther leaned back in his chair, crossed his arms over his chest, and stared at the phone on his desk. It was on speaker because he hated having that blasted thing stuck to his ear to talk. His office door was closed to keep out anyone who might want to pry, and he had a scrambler on the phone so the call couldn't be traced to his location.

"Are we clear about what I want?"

The crunch of chips echoed through the phone lines. He pictured the caller wiping off the grease on his jeans. "Ya, dude. I can leak that information no sweat."

Gunther relaxed his muscles and leaned forward, bringing his mouth close to the speaker. "Especially to Russia. They must think the U.S. is planning something. Nothing specific, mind you, very general."

"Relax, dude. I know what I'm doing. You think that political scandal three months ago happened by itself?"

Gunther searched his memory for the events his hacker spoke of, but he'd still been in limbo then. He had to take the guy's word for it.

"Just get it done."

"As long as you pay me, dude, I'll leak or hack whatever you want."

"Excellent. I'll be in touch."

He hit the button to hang up the phone. It had taken time to find an unethical hacker skilled enough to do what he wanted. If he'd had a soul, it would have been even harder. Score another one for Death's almost purge of the souls in purgatory.

He smiled. Things were going along swimmingly. He could almost taste the wars that would erupt once he was finished.

Without a knock, his door swung open. Conquest moseyed inside and threw himself into the chair in front of Gunther's desk.

"Why the smile? What has you so happy?" Conquest asked.

"Plans are in motion for war. Maybe even more than one. Strings for more than just a few superpowers are being pulled."

"Nice."

"When will Famine be here?" Gunther sat straighter, hands folded on his desk.

Conquest shrugged. "The priest has a timetable. He needs to restore his energy before summoning our brother. He was thrown off by having to summon me again."

With strategy came patience. Gunther took a deep breath and let it out slowly. As long as they were all reunited, he could wait for the priest's schedule. "Fine. How are things going at the lab?"

A flash of worry crossed Conquest's face, but he smiled. "On track. Paperwork says we're creating and testing a flu vaccine. It's taking a lot of magic, but all the lab people think that's what they're doing too. Creating a new vaccine because the previous one doesn't work. But this virus they're creating will be one hundred times more virulent than the flu."

Gunther steepled his fingers under his chin. "Good. And there's a plan to infect the population?"

Conquest gave him a withering look. "Of course. But we may have a problem. One of the angels was there yesterday asking questions."

"They were at the lab?"

"Yeah, that reporter for CTBN. I don't know what she knows yet, but I can find out."

"I'm not worried, but keep an eye on her. They can't stop what's coming."

Even if the angels could slow it down, it wouldn't be enough. The apocalypse was coming and most of the population was going to die.

Late Wednesday morning, Becky sat at her desk at the television station, putting final touches on stories she needed to send to Ellen for approval. The floor hummed with conversation, phones ringing, the chug of the photo copier in the print room a few feet away from her office. It wasn't like the hustle and bustle of a newsroom from TV shows she'd seen since arriving on Earth. Or ones she'd planted memories of. It was the reality of hundreds of people creating news for a bustling city. Louder, more intense, faster chatter than before Victor had gone to jail. Everyone was working on something, almost all of them stories about violence and criminal activity in the city. The puff pieces were a thing of the past. Those palate cleansers after the horror and gore were gone. Fewer of them were happening, but there were more stories the people of Toronto needed to know about to keep them safe.

Besides the notes she was compiling for an eventual story based on the tips she'd been getting, she was also working on follow-ups to the gang activity in the city. It had been down for a few weeks while Victor was in jail, but it was on the rise again. And her continuing series about the horrible way people were treating each other these days. Those stories they had in spades.

Missing information gnawed at her. She picked up her phone and called Rachel's number at the station.

"Detective Malak." The clipped, yet professional tone of Rachel's voice was somehow annoying.

"Hey. I know you're probably busy, but did you have an update on Karl Bishop's murder? Any leads you can tell me about?"

A sigh on the other end rankled Becky's nerves. If the call had been from any other reporter, Rachel would be all smiles and eager to help even if she had nothing to say.

"We have no leads on the case right now. No suspects. If we get anything more, our corporate communications officer will inform the media."

"Thanks." She stopped herself from saying "for nothing".

"No problem."

She chatted a little more, asking about non work stuff, to get Rachel to relax a little. The angel was always on, always ready to shoot down anything Becky needed. If she kept it light, maybe Rachel would start treating her better. She'd said she would try, but for some reason, it was ingrained in her to push Becky's buttons. They were more like sisters than they'd originally realized.

She hung up with Rachel and called Sarah's number to

get an update on the pawnshop owner. He was doing well after surgery.

After her call to Sarah, she looked at the pile of stuff on her desk that Laura had left her, with photos of Dr. Althaus on top. Where there was one reaper, there were more. How many others would she find if she searched old pictures?

Instead of doing the research herself—it was far too big a job for one person—she fired off an email to all the interns, asking them to pull photos from everywhere for all the people in the committee, people in all levels of government, higher-ups in the military, people with prominent positions, but not in the spotlight. She asked for any pictures of anyone who showed up as a blur in the photo. From random crowds all over the world. As far back as they could find. Then she asked for them to circle all the people who were blurry to them and bring the printed photos to her office.

While they tackled that job, she pulled up her email inbox to respond to messages. It was a light day for emails, so it only took her an hour to get through them all.

With one job complete, she turned to gathering information about the people who would be at the peace talks in Ottawa. Background research was key to having a good interview with people. Since she'd given the intern pool a huge job with the photos, she tackled this research on her own, pulling up information about the delegates, printing bios, and jotting down questions she wanted to ask given the opportunity.

Another twinge of guilt twisted her stomach. Kevin Moore should be the one going to Ottawa to cover the talks. Snatching the senior anchor position away from him with magic was a rotten thing to do, and maybe when this was over, she'd fix it before going home, busting herself to intern where she should have been. But right now, she was where she needed to be.

In need of caffeine, she dashed to the break area, poured a coffee, then added three sugars and a generous amount of cream. On her way back to her office, Laura popped up in her cubicle.

"We have lots of pictures for you."

Becky jerked her head toward her office. "Gather what you have and meet me in my office."

Sipping her coffee, Becky contemplated what the interns would show her. Back behind her desk, she cleared off the surface as much as possible, unsure how many stacks of papers they would bring. She'd given them a huge task, so she was expecting lots of print-outs. Later, when time permitted and the weather allowed, she would plant a few trees to make up for it.

A line of interns slowly filed into her office. Each had stacks of paper spilling out of their arms. One of them held the stack in place with her chin. Laura rolled a supply cart through the door, stacks of paper on the top and bottom.

"Wow, that's a lot."

Laura nodded. "We put them in date order."

With the help of the other interns, Laura emptied the cart, putting the stacks on any available surface in the office. Some went on the corners of Becky's desk. Others on the credenza against the back wall. The remaining piles went on Kevin Moore's desk and chair.

Laura pointed out the stacks on the credenza. "Those are from the late 1800s to early 1950s. The ones on Kevin's desk are late 1950s to early 1990s. And you have late 1990s to current. We've also noted on them where in the world the pictures came from."

"Thanks for all the hard work on this."

The interns left, confusion settled on their faces, but they didn't ask what it was all for.

Laura sat in the chair in front of Becky's desk, the centre purposely left free of paper. "Do you want any help going through all this stuff?"

"No, that's okay. You've done so much work already."

Laura nodded and left.

A niggling of regret tugged at her conscious. After all this work, she usually let Laura in on what she was looking for, what she intended to prove. But she couldn't tell her intern about the apocalypse and the fact that reapers were probably here in greater numbers than ever. Would Laura believe her if she had told her? Or would the intern question her ability to do her job?

Becky immediately went for the pile from the fifties, plopping it on her desk. Flipping through the stack, she stopped at the first circle that indicated the person was blurry. As predicted, they were not blurry for her. She continued going through the pile. There weren't a lot of blurry people in the fifties. At least not in photos captured and transferred to the internet. How many photos were out there that hadn't somehow made their way to the internet?

The next pile she went through was from the 1920s. A smattering of them had blurs.

She picked the stack that included photos from 1914 to 1918. Lots of blurs on each page made sense because of the war. Reapers would have been out in full force to assist the fallen soldiers on their journey.

Rummaging through another stack, she pulled out the photos from the Second World War. Unsurprisingly, there were a lot of blurs there too, especially in pictures from Europe.

She grabbed another pile. The most recent photos, including those of a world addicted to social media and selfies. She shuffled through them quickly, disheartened by the amount of circles on each page. But they weren't concentrated in one place or the other. There were a lot in Russia and the U.S., especially near the Canadian border. But there were almost as many in pictures from Canada, Europe, Asia, Australia. There were even a few from Antarctica.

She took a deep breath and put the papers down. There were way more reapers now than in the other pictures centred around mass casualties.

A bad feeling gnawed in the pit of her stomach.

She got up and shut her office door. Before going back to her desk, she closed the blinds to shut out prying eyes. General curiosity was the nature of the business and she didn't want anyone speculating on what she was talking about or who she was talking with if the conversation got heated.

Instead of using her work phone, she pulled out her cell phone, dialing each angel one at a time.

"What's up? I've got work to do," Rachel said.

Sarah shushed her. "We all have work to do. Becky wouldn't call us if it wasn't important."

"Did you find out more from your tipster?" Leah asked.

Becky filled them in on the reaper situation.

"Got your interns to do the heavy lifting again, huh?" Rachel said.

Becky tapped her foot and sighed. "I had other things to work on. Bottom line, there are easily ten times more reapers here than there should be. They are getting ready for mass casualties. It's happening soon."

On edge Wednesday evening, Becky dropped her purse and computer bag on the table by the door to the loft, then paced in front of the windows instead of sitting on the comfortable, welcoming sofa.

It was training night for Darla and her friends, but the last thing Becky wanted was going through self-defence moves. At least for Darla's group the swords didn't need to be brought out. The loft was empty. Rachel, Sarah, and Leah probably waited in the basement for her to arrive. The sex workers would already be there, too. They were prompt. Especially when any delays meant fewer johns for the night.

Becky took a deep breath, then padded to her room to change. On her way through the kitchen, she grabbed a bottle of water from the fridge.

As she suspected, everyone lounged on the benches in the training room, waiting for her. Rachel huffed.

"It's about time. I was about to start without you."

Becky nodded, stepping to the centre of the room. "I apologize for the delay. Let's get started."

The air hung heavy with anticipation as the fallen angels lined up in front of the women. Leah laid out the evening's agenda.

"We're going to start with a few basics. First, we'll show you how to block a punch, then a kick. Following that, we'll demonstrate a few simple holds and escapes you can use to protect yourself in the event of an attack."

The women watched intently as Rachel, Sarah, and Leah took turns demonstrating each technique. Once the basics were covered, Becky stepped forward.

"Okay, now it's your turn. We'll pair you up with someone close to your size and you'll practise on each other. You'll be going through these moves so much that you can do them without thought. Ready?"

The women nodded, some with more enthusiasm than others, and paired off. Rachel, Becky, and Leah moved around the room, providing guidance and encouragement as the women practiced. Sarah left the gym, mumbling something about making dinner. Becky's stomach grumbled at the mere mention of food. Workouts always gave her an appetite.

After an hour of practice, Leah clapped her hands to get the women's attention. "All right, that's enough for tonight. We're going to end with a few breathing exercises to help you stay calm in stressful situations."

The women gathered around Leah and practiced the breathing exercises she taught them. By the time they were finished, the women were visibly more relaxed and confident.

Rachel stepped forward and gave the women a nod of approval. "Good work, everyone. We'll see you next week."

The women thanked the fallen angels and left the gym, each of them with a new sense of empowerment. Becky smiled as she watched them go, proud of what they had accomplished.

Chapter Ten

Energized from the workout, Becky dashed into the loft before Rachel and Leah, beelining for the sofa. She grabbed the television remote and put it on the twenty-four-hour news channel. The place smelled amazing, with hints of garlic and ginger hanging in the air. Sarah stood in front of the stove, stirring something.

Becky's contentment crashed. The breaking news scrolling along the bottom of the screen reported an earthquake in Wavecrest, a small town near Niagara Falls.

Becky flicked the television off and was already at the door when her cell phone rang. "I'm on my way," she said to her boss.

"Make it fast. We want you on location."

"Sorry, Sarah. Won't be able to eat dinner." Becky grabbed her purse and dashed out the door.

She raced across town in record time, grabbed directions to the earthquake site, and flashed a quick smile to her driver and cameraman, Henry. The boom operator, Owen, piled into the back of the station's white van. She'd worked with both of them before but never on something like this. Reports were already coming in about numerous casualties in the small town.

The two-hour drive took an hour and a half with Henry standing on the accelerator. Flood lights surrounded the area, turning night into day and highlighting the pile of rubble that was once the middle of town. Small fires dotted the surrounding area. Smoke rose from the burning buildings, spiralling into the air. Small crowds of people, three and four to a group, gathered, hugging each other, crying.

Rescue workers emerged from what looked like the town's city hall, carrying a gurney. Becky focused on the unmoving man they carried out. Covered in dirt and debris, he looked like he had been buried alive. The building crumbled some more, another wall crashing to the ground. How could anyone survive that? For the first time since being exiled, she asked why she had to endure this? The suffering was too much. How could she handle not being able to help any of these people?

The man moved a hand, coughed. Hope sprang within her again.

"Let's set up over here," she said, pointing to a spot in the centre of town that looked safe.

Her crew followed her as she picked her way through the debris. She took a deep breath and plastered a sombre look on her face. When the red light went on, she rattled off the usual spiel that gave some information but not all of it. As soon as the light went off, she let out a sigh. She needed to talk to the rescue workers to find out about casualties.

"Stay here and set up the next shot, please. I'm going to see if I can find someone in authority."

Her crew did as she asked, and she walked through the piles of rubble to the town hall. From the looks of it, the most devastated by the quake, it lay in a shambles. Sparks flew from the crashed building. Smoke rose from the centre. Most of the crowds of people huddled on the sidewalk leading to the building.

A group of people off to the side, well back from the building, caught her attention. The majority of them with hard hats and heavy boots screamed construction workers. But in the middle of the group, a tall man with an army uniform and stern expression spoke to one man who looked a little too well dressed for construction. Despite the distance between them, Becky's stomach knotted. From here, she could smell the souled and soulless, but the army guy didn't make a blip on her radar. It was impossible to get a look at his arm to see if he bore the tattoo of War, but she didn't need to see it to know. War was here in Wavecrest.

From the way he spoke to the construction crew, they were building something for him. Later, she would investigate that, see if any new permits had been issued lately. While construction during the winter was rare, it wasn't impossible.

Right now, she needed to help the people of the town, and that meant getting information out there.

She found a policeman protecting a caution tape line, blocking people from approaching City Hall.

"Hi, constable. I'm Becky Malak from CTBN. I'm so sorry about all of this. How can my viewers help?"

The constable looked at her and barely cracked a cursory smile. Not that she blamed him. Earthquakes were nothing to smile at. She would stay as long as she needed to, as long as she could do something to help.

"We need to find the missing. There's a list started over there." He pointed to what looked like the library. "We just don't have the manpower. We're a small-town. Half of it is missing. The quake hit just before everyone at work would be leaving for the day."

She took off her jacket, unclipped her microphone, and rolled up her sleeves. "Where do you need me?"

He looked at her for the first time, really looked at her. Perfectly coiffed hair. Makeup fit for the camera. Pristine white blouse. At least she'd worn dress slacks instead of a skirt.

"You're probably best behind the camera."

His condescension rankled her. "You said you needed help. I can help. You'd turn down help because I'm not wearing the right clothes?"

"I'd turn you down because it's not safe yet. We're still having aftershocks."

As if to prove his point, a shock wave went through the town. The earth seemed to tilt on her. The ground shook. A crack appeared in the middle of the road just in front of the town hall. From her left, a crash sounded as another building collapsed. Shouts from the town hall rang through the air as rescue personnel rushed to safety points.

She managed to keep her balance, riding the wave until it finally stopped. As the street quieted again, she heard a small whimper. Faint, almost indiscernible, it came from the building that had just collapsed.

"Do you hear that?"

"Hear what?"

She listened harder. The whimpering grew louder, turning into soft sobs. "That crying."

"What crying?"

He couldn't hear it? Why couldn't he hear it? It didn't matter why. She heard it and she couldn't do nothing. She raced over to the building. Before she could disappear into the rubble, the constable grabbed her arm.

"What do you think you're doing?"

"I hear someone crying in there."

"Even if that was true, you have no protective gear, no training."

He had a point. But she had to believe that she wouldn't be here if she wasn't meant to help. She had to get in that building. She wouldn't be hearing someone crying if she shouldn't go in and save them.

"I have a segment to air."

She marched over to her crew. "Henry, we need to do a thirty-second segment, then I need you guys to distract Constable Fraser over there."

"What are you going to do?" Owen asked.

"You shouldn't ask questions you don't really want the answer to."

For the constable, she made a show of doing her segment. When the thirty seconds were over, he had already lost interest and returned to the caution tape he'd been guarding before.

"What do we have in the van that I can use?"

"Use for what, Becky? You still haven't told us what you intend to do."

"Never mind. Can you mill around over there?" She pointed to the town square. "I need to do something."

They both shrugged but knew better than to argue with her. If she turned on the angelic power of persuasion, they would do almost anything she asked. Almost. The power of persuasion couldn't make them do something against their moral compass. She'd never had to use it. And she hoped she never did. She much preferred when they came around to her way of thinking on their own because it was the right thing to do.

When her crew left her, she rummaged in the back of the van. She found a black, plastic flashlight. She switched it on to make sure it worked. With the flashlight's help, she rummaged through more of the boxes in the back. She found some rope and grabbed that too.

With her gaze on the constable, she made her way back to the building. She went around the back, away from prying eyes and overprotective police constables. Where the building had collapsed, she found a small opening just big enough for her to fit through.

She cupped her hands around her mouth and said, "Hello? Is anyone there?"

It seemed like minutes passed, but it was only seconds before a small sob answered her. She couldn't tell if it was from a male or a female. Couldn't tell if they were old or young. The only thing she could determine at that precise moment was that they were alive, for now, and they were scared.

She squeezed into the opening and turned on the flashlight. A swath of light slashed through the darkness. She summoned all the angel power she had. Her wings started to glow, lighting the way through the debris.

"Are you there? I'm coming to help you."

"I'm here," a small voice sounded from the darkness in front of her.

Her heart lurched in her chest. The sound of a small child. What were they doing in there by themselves? Everyone had been evacuated when the first quake struck.

"What's your name?"

When the child didn't answer right away, panic gripped Becky. Was she too late? She would never forgive the constable if she lost the child. She pressed further into the building.

"Ashley."

"That's a nice name. Can you keep talking to me, Ashley? I need to follow the sound of your voice."

"I can sing a song."

"Okay, that's good. Sing a song."

"What should I sing?"

Becky searched her planted memories for a child's song. "How about Itsy Bitsy Spider? Do you know that one?"

"Yes. I can sing that," Ashley said.

As the child's warbles reached her, Becky turned right. The voice got louder. She kept going until the child's voice seemed to surround her. She was in the front of the building, piles of rock and rubble surrounding her.

"Where are you?"

From the corner, fingers emerged from a pile of rocks. Becky's heart raced. She summoned all of her strength and angel powers and tossed the small boulders away. Underneath a sturdy wood table, a little girl crouched against the wall. Becky reached her hand in. The girl grabbed it tightly and rushed into Becky's arms.

"Hi, I'm Becky," she said, brushing a lock of hair away from the girl's dirty face.

Ashley beamed at her. "Hi. Are you an angel?"

Panic raced through her. Could the child see her wings? She'd turned off the illumination as soon as she started digging her out. "Why do you ask, sweetie?"

"Because Mama said angels are always watching over us. And you're here saving me."

She shifted the girl to her other hip as she navigated the short distance to the front of the building. The structure still held most of its weight, but there was no telling when it would buckle. They had to get out of there soon.

"I'm just a reporter for the local TV station, sweetie."

She shoved rocks aside, hoping Ashley didn't realize she shouldn't be strong enough to do that. No one person would be strong enough to clear a path to the front door.

The child didn't seem to notice. She just smiled as she snuggled into Becky's neck.

The light almost blinded her when they emerged from the building.

"A little help over here, please!"

Shouts and pounding footsteps followed her plea. Within seconds, someone whisked the girl out of her arms and wrapped a blanket around her. A woman, tears streaking down her cheeks, let out a sob and rushed over to the child. She scooped her into her arms and planted kisses all over the child's face.

Becky smiled, then collapsed onto the curb. Man, she was tired. Using all her powers at once really drained her. Someone draped an orange blanket around her shoulders.

"What were you thinking?"

She raised a hand to her eyes to block out the flood lights as she looked up into the disapproving face of Constable Fraser. "I was thinking I couldn't ignore the sound of someone sobbing in a collapsed building."

A tingle went through her wings. The tiredness she felt lifted, and the scrapes on her hands stopped stinging.

He took her elbow and urged her to stand. "It was stupid to put yourself at risk like that. We would have found her."

"Yeah, and what if you found her too late? You didn't even hear her crying."

"True. How did you hear her?"

Better change the subject before he started to pry even more. "Was that her mother?"

"Yes, she's been frantic since the first quake. At least that's one missing we can cross off the list and move to the found column."

"He's right, you know."

Becky jerked her head around at Sarah's voice.

"What are you doing here?"

Sarah handed her a bottle of water. "The town put out a call for doctors right after it happened. I got here while you were in there." She pointed to the destroyed building.

"I'm glad you're here. There's so much devastation."

"There is. But you need to be more careful."

Becky glanced over at the mother who was still holding her child like she'd never let her go again. "I couldn't ignore her."

Sarah peered over her shoulder. The police constable had walked back over to the caution tape. "How did you hear her?"

Becky shrugged. "Angel radio?"

Sarah walked behind her and let out a low whistle. "You have a lot of power back. How? Didn't you use any to get the girl out?"

"I've been getting a lot of power back. I thought I used a lot to get her out. Maybe I didn't use as much as I thought."

"Good. Rachel would have been pissed that you weren't conserving it."

"That is the least of our worries." She pointed to the army guy. "War is here."

Sarah frowned. "We'll figure out why later. You should rest a bit. I'll go see where they need me."

Becky watched Sarah dash off through the emergency responders before standing and taking a deep breath. She picked her way through the rubble to find her crew again. She fixed her makeup, smoothed out her hair, and didn't have to fake the serious expression on her face. After giving an impassioned plea to her viewers to send coats, clothes, food, and anything else they could to help, she signed off and joined the people helping to find survivors.

War stood amidst the rubble of the construction site, his eyes scanning the destruction with a mix of frustration and anger. He had spent so much time and effort to find the perfect location to build his bunker, only for it to be ruined by an unexpected earthquake. He knew he needed to find a new site quickly, but first he needed to deal with the two fallen angels on scene.

As he turned, he saw them—that reporter and the doctor, both looking at the wreckage with horrified expressions. The other one, the detective, didn't appear to be around.

He thought about approaching them, his eyes fixed on Becky as she noticed the construction site. He knew she was intelligent, and he didn't want her to put the pieces together too soon. But he didn't want to give away anything by getting too close to her. If she didn't already know who he was, she would find out soon enough. And the longer it took, the better for him and the grand plan.

His mind raced with plans to secure a new site and make it seem like the construction had always been intended for that location. He needed to tap into more magic to make that happen, but he was confident he could do it.

While he watched the angels, he made a quick call to Conquest.

"Angels are in Wavecrest."

Conquest sighed. "Shit. Not that it will do much good."

"No, but we can't continue building here. I've got some ideas of where else we can move the bunker to."

He gathered information from Conquest about how the gangs were doing in the city, wreaking more havoc with

Caleb at the helm. A few minutes later, he concluded the call, shoving his phone back into his pocket.

War strode off, his mind already focused on the next steps in his plan. A little earthquake may have gotten in his way, but he was not one to be deterred. He was War, one of the four horsemen of the apocalypse, and he would stop at nothing to achieve his goals.

The next morning, Becky woke to the smell of coffee coming from the motel room's coffee maker. The curtains were pulled open, giving a view of the small parking lot. It was full of cars belonging to people who had come to the town to help out. Thankfully, the second news of the earthquake hit Ellen's desk, her producer had booked two rooms at the motel. Upon checking in last night she'd been informed they were all booked up, so Sarah stayed in Becky's room.

The second bed was empty, freshly made as if Sarah hadn't slept there. Aftershocks had kept both of them up well past midnight. How was Sarah up and out already?

At least there was coffee.

Becky threw the covers aside, stretched, and got out of bed. Before doing anything else, she poured herself a cup of lukewarm coffee, sprinkled in a few creamer packets, and added enough sugar to give her a jolt. She gulped down the contents of the paper cup with a grimace. It tasted burnt, too strong, and wasn't hot enough. But the caffeine was needed. Her next cup would be a proper one from a coffee shop, if the one in town was still operational.

After tossing the empty cup in the trash can, she padded to the bathroom and did a quick check of her wings. Surprised to see lots of white, she made a mental note to add this information to her spreadsheet. Sarah had said she still had lots of power, but Becky's wings were almost completely white now. The spots of black were tiny dots peppered throughout her limbs.

A refreshing shower and clean clothes chased the rest of the sleepiness away. The power she had explained why her arms didn't feel like lead weights, why her legs didn't scream in pain with each movement, why the scratches on her hands had disappeared.

After rescuing Ashley, she didn't think she'd be able to move for a week. She'd expected to be a bundle of sore muscles today in need of a soak in a hot tub. But she could run a marathon without breaking a sweat.

She dug in her purse and pulled out her phone. She called her crew to tell them to be ready in an hour. She wanted to do another segment on the earthquake and try to drum up more help for the town.

To prepare for the segment, she pulled out her laptop, connected to the motel's Wi-Fi, and keyed in some searches for tectonic activity in the area. Based on the information from various articles, the most severe earthquake to happen in the area registered a three on the Richter scale. The strength of yesterday's quake hadn't been confirmed yet, but rumours floated around that it was a seven. Frowning, she pushed the laptop away.

Her phone buzzed with a text message.

Gunther Fertig was in Wavecrest before the earthquake.

X

She pulled the laptop back and did a search for Gunther. She'd assumed he was here with other military personnel to help keep order in the town because of the disaster. Why had he been here before anything had happened?

The construction project was obviously military, but why do it now? There were no military bases in Wavecrest. Nothing interesting popped up on the search for Gunther. She switched gears, used a little angel power pointed at the computer, and did a search for permits in the area.

A permit for a building on the edge of town came up. A building big enough to be a bunker and the plans indicated it would be underground. It was issued last week.

She had some time before she needed to meet her crew. She gathered her things, stuffing her laptop in a bag. With the amount of power she had back, she didn't need a coat to keep out the chill, but she donned one anyway. Warmer than usual, the weather could turn at any moment and she didn't have time to answer questions about whether she was cold or not.

She slung the laptop bag over her shoulder, grabbed her room key from the desk, and rushed out of the room, turning the door hanger to Do Not Disturb.

Work was underway throughout the town, moving toppled concrete, moving crushed cars, moving crumbled bricks. Rescue workers still checked the rubble to make sure they'd located everyone. She stopped at the board holding the missing list. Her heart sank when she saw the number of people still missing and the number of people dead.

With a population of a little over twenty-five hundred people, almost a quarter of those were dead or missing. How many more people would be lost before they stopped the apocalypse? She had no doubts that this disaster was a sign of the coming end.

She picked her way through the town as quickly as she could until she reached the construction site. Despite the tragedy, a foreman was still on duty. She used a spark of power to unlock the gate, pushed it open, and sauntered through.

A quick glance at the hole in the ground a hundred feet away from the office confirmed they'd already started digging.

The man walked toward her, his thick coat, unzipped, flapping in the breeze. A yellow hard hat covered his head. The stern expression on his face reminded her of Rachel's disapproval every time Becky's job was mentioned.

"You can't be here." He pointed toward the gate. "You'll have to leave."

Ignoring his comment, she stepped closer to him, a confident smile on her face. "I'm here from CTBN. What are you building there? How far down is it?"

His face turned red. Pursed lips turned white. "That's none of your business. Get out."

The permit said they were digging eight feet deep. She inched closer to the hole, then darted over, stopping at the rim. Peering down into the darkness, she gasped as a wave of vertigo hit her. If that was eight feet, she was a demon. It looked to be deeper than twelve feet. Closer to twenty.

A hand around her arm startled her. Heart racing, she pulled her arm out of the foreman's grasp.

"You can't be here."

The foreman nudged her forcefully toward the gate. It clanged shut behind her, the foreman mumbling under his breath about trespassers.

She raced back to the hotel room, pulled out her laptop, and did a search for tectonic plates and earthquake zones in Southwestern Ontario. A heat-style map showed all the likely spots in the province for tectonic activity, with the highest severity being a three in Wavecrest. Based on the devastation, the earthquake to hit the town was a lot higher than a three. The rumours about a seven were probably true.

She called Laura.

When the intern answered, Becky relaxed. "Good morning. Can you get me confirmation of the severity of the earthquake here in Wavecrest?"

"No problem. Do you want to wait or do you want me to call you back?"

Becky checked the time. She needed to meet her crew in front of city hall in fifteen minutes.

"I'll wait if you don't mind."

"Okay, hold on." The sound of fingers clacking over a keyboard drifted through the phone line. Then hold music.

A few moments later, Laura returned. "Experts say it was a seven."

"Thanks."

She ended the call—Laura would understand the lack of small talk—and shoved her laptop into the bag again. It couldn't be a coincidence with the digging, War being there, and the severity of the earthquake. Quakes that high on the scale weren't unheard of in the area, but they were highly unlikely.

The passage came back to her about weapons in the land. Was the earthquake part of a prophecy? That meant the final signs would happen soon. They had to gather everything they needed to summon War and send him back. She'd get a better idea at the peace talks where the world stood with the apocalypse, but the churning of her stomach told her it wasn't good.

Chapter Eleven

Settled into her hotel room in downtown Ottawa Friday morning, Becky sat at the desk by the window with her laptop open. She had the curtains pulled wide so she could enjoy the view of the city. On the desk beside her computer and scattered all over the second double bed in the room, were the pictures the interns had printed for her a few days ago.

Every instinct in her body told her she needed to be at the peace talks that would be starting Monday, but she wanted to be back in Wavecrest helping the people of the town recover. Sarah had stayed another day to help out. After two more sixty-second spots for the news, the town had plenty of help arriving in the form of volunteers and supplies.

An empty plate from her lunch needed to be put outside the room so hotel staff could take it away. Looking at the crumbs made her want a snack even though she wasn't hungry. She pushed herself out of the chair, grabbed the plate, then put it outside the door.

She took a bottle of water from the mini bar, cracked it

open, and sat at the desk again. The station could pay for one bottle of water. They'd given her an expense allowance, but she didn't want to blow through all of it since she didn't need to eat that much now that she had a lot more power in her wings. But she didn't want to draw any sort of suspicion by not having anything to expense either.

Stationed at the desk again, she shuffled through the papers, looking for pictures of people who were expected at the peace talks. She pulled out the ones she found and put them in a separate pile on the desk. Most of the pages had multiple circles on them.

One of the delegates, showing in some pictures as being from Iran, showed in more recent photos as being from Iraq with a different name. Becky opened a web browser and searched for the person, going back as far as she could with an image search once she found a decent digital picture. She found the same person in photos from the 1950s looking the same age as they looked now.

She had no doubts they were a reaper. A bad feeling churned in her stomach. Maybe she should have had another snack to settle her.

How many reapers would be at the peace talks? The apocalypse was already underway when they'd arrived on Earth. Maybe this summit was what was going to tip the scales.

Without a lot of time to do more research, she shoved the thoughts of doom and gloom aside. She had to meet Henry downstairs in a few minutes to scope out the ballroom where the talks were going to be held. Then she had to prepare for the welcome dinner later that night.

She pulled up her email, scanned the subject lines, and dismissed most of them as being able to wait until later. But the one from Laura about the lab required immediate attention. She opened the message. Laura was looking into the lab some more and previous vaccines the lab created. She was also doing more research on the microbiologist. Becky admired her drive but didn't think she'd find much on the doctor. If she was right, and the doctor was a reaper, there would be an ironclad history laid out.

Becky fired off an email back, thanking her for her diligence and telling her not to work too late.

She closed the laptop and grabbed her purse, making sure her room key was tucked into one of the inside pockets, then put the doorknob hanger to Do Not Disturb and left the room in search of Henry.

Unaccustomed to wearing a dress, Becky smoothed the back of hers every few steps to make sure the skirt was still around her legs. Each step sent a wisp of air across her legs, making her feel like she was walking around in her underwear. The heels she wore were also new to her. Higher than most of the shoes she wore, the heels squished her toes and made the pads of her feet hurt.

Why did women torture themselves this way?

She found Henry already in the ballroom at the table for various TV networks. At the table with him were on screen talent for two other major networks for the country.

As she approached the table, Henry's eyes lit up. "You look amazing. Gorgeous even."

Heat rushed to her cheeks and she grinned like a schoolgirl. "Thank you. You don't look bad yourself."

Henry wore a black suit, with a crisp white shirt and a splash of colour with a teal tie. The rest of the group was attired similarly.

The gazes of some of the delegates nearby, as well as

those from the table made her rethink the torture question. She could see why once in a while someone might want to dress up.

The table for the reporters was at the front of the ball-room, in a second row of tables. The first row was for over-flow of the delegates that didn't fit into the high table. At the front of the ballroom a high table had been set up like there was a wedding going on. Name tags, written in gold ink on stark white cards, placed the most important dele-gates from Iran and Iraq on opposite ends of the long table. In the middle, as a buffer, the arbitrators assigned by the United Alliance of Countries sat with their hands folded in front of them.

Becky did a slow turn in her spot to see where everyone else was sitting as people trickled into the room. She craned her neck in search of War, but he wasn't there yet.

The room filled up quickly. The delegates wouldn't enter until everyone was present and seated. When all the surrounding seats were filled, a hush fell over the room. Delegates from the neighbouring countries strode into the room, each country taking the side of the room that matched their side of the table.

Becky sat up in her chair, scanning the crowd again, and was dismayed to see War sitting at a table in the front, centre, with politicians and overflow delegates from Iran.

He turned as if sensing her stare. When his gaze found her, he grinned, then leaned over to speak to the delegate from Iran sitting beside him.

Her fingers twitched. She contemplated using her power to separate them. But she couldn't waste what she had. She was closer to figuring out how to get more back—her spreadsheet had enough data by now to analyze—but would she have time and opportunity over the weekend to work on that? If something happened at the talks, she wouldn't have enough power to save everyone if she squandered power now.

For the most part, she listened with half an ear to the inane small talk going around the table. She replied at the appropriate times when one of the other reporters asked a question, but she kept her focus on the head table. It would make things easier to figure out if she knew how many people in the room had souls. Based on her analysis of her own table, only one person had one. The senior anchor for WorldWideNews.

Once dinner was served and they were permitted to walk around the room, she shot out of her chair, making an excuse about going to the ladies' room. Instead of leaving the ballroom, she did a circuit of the space, starting at the head table and working her way through the rest of the crowd. In a room that currently contained two hundred people, only a handful had souls. The arbitrator for the talks was among the souled and gave her some relief. The rest comprised of a few delegates from UN member countries, the on-air talent from her own table she'd already known about, and another reporter from an online newspaper. Most of the souled were over seventy at least, based on appearances only. Until she did research on each person, she didn't know for sure how old they were. There were two who looked to be younger.

What disturbed her the most wasn't the lack of souls in the room. She expected that based on Death's purge of souls from purgatory. What worried her was the number of people who gave off nothing. Not souled or soulless, but something in between. Some of them matched the pictures she'd looked at before coming down for dinner. Laura and the intern team had done a great job of finding people she suspected were reapers even though they had no idea that's what they'd been looking for.

But there were people in the crowd who weren't in any of the pictures her team had found. A lot of reapers present could mean a breakdown of the talks would happen here. It could mean nothing. Maybe they just happened to be the delegates assigned to be here and everything would go smoothly.

Somehow she doubted there was no cause for alarm. Especially because War was there and currently bending the ear of another delegate, this one from Iraq.

She wished she knew what he was saying. Every so often, he would look up at her and grin, then go back to talking to the person. What lies was he whispering in their ears? His only goal was war. Was he planting the seeds for more than Iran and Iraq to declare war on each other? So many countries were present. With the most fragile of alliances between some nations, it would be easy for War to tip the scales. Convince a delegate it was in their country's best interest to start a conflict with another country.

She sighed on the way back to her table. She should eat and get a good sleep. It was going to be a very long weekend.

Chapter Twelve

After a weekend of breathlessness and a pounding heart, Becky and Henry were finally setting up for their broadcasts in the huge hallway outside the ballroom where the peace talks would be happening. Beside the ballroom, the room they'd had the welcome dinner in had been transformed into part lounge, part green room complete with refreshments for the press.

The tension in the air made Becky's hair rise on the back of her neck. After the dinner on Friday, everyone seemed to be getting along. There had been no harsh words, no arguing. The tone had been set. But over the weekend, little skirmishes had erupted in areas all over the hotel when opposite sides of the conflict mingled. The hotel had ended up closing the pool and the bar to all attendees of the talks, including the press.

Chatter floated in the air as each TV station set up their cameras, figuring out shots.

Flashbulbs popped when the arbitrator arrived. He gave a slight nod to each camera pointed his way but gave no expression. His lips were a firm line, his jaw tense. He pulled the handle on the ballroom door and disappeared inside.

A few minutes later, the delegates from Iran and Iraq arrived. Surrounded by bodyguards, each delegate gave the same non-expression to the cameras before they entered the ballroom.

Shortly after the delegates, the translators arrived. Becky spotted a new one in the mix who was not in the photos she saw from the Prague talks. She inched closer to the group of translators to see if she could detect a soul. Nothing came back to her. Another reaper.

Her stomach lurched. One more reaper in the mix couldn't be good. Before she could dwell on Death's helper, War arrived. Unlike the others attending the talks, his expression told her a lot. His eyes sparkled. His lips were turned up into a grin. He waved at the crowd of reporters, then ducked into the room.

Shit.

There was no way security would let her into the ballroom even with a press pass. Not until they did photo ops later just before the lunch break.

The mischief in War's eyes set her nerves on edge.

Using her powers was an option. She had enough that she could convince security she was a delegate and should be in the room. But she couldn't risk it. There was no guarantee she wouldn't lose it all. Not losing all her power after using it at the site of the earthquake might have been a fluke. She needed to find time to analyze her spreadsheet.

Henry waved his hand to get her attention. "Ready to do the opening bite?"

She nodded. "We'll do a quick one now and hopefully have good news to report after lunch."

While she readied herself to go on-air, the other

reporters did the same. She gave her spiel, making sure to keep her voice even and expression neutral.

When the red light went off, she let out a sigh. She needed coffee and a snack. Even though she wasn't hungry, she found eating food comforting, especially if it was sugary.

In the green room, her stomach remained clenched the entire morning while she made small talk with the other reporters. None of them had any idea what the stakes actually were. Sure, they thought war might break out in Iran and Iraq, but most probably figured those countries were too far away to affect what happened in North America. How wrong they were. But with the added threat of War whispering in the ears of other countries known for local disputes, multiple wars could affect most of the planet.

When lunch was announced, she grabbed Henry and beelined for the hallway.

The smiling delegates cleared some of the butterflies in her stomach. Then War emerged, his smile even broader than the one he'd had going into the talks. That couldn't be a good thing.

Before the parties left for lunch, they posed for pictures but answered no questions except to say the talks were going well. They'd started out that way in Prague too.

After Becky finished wrapping a follow-up segment for the talks, her phone buzzed.

She stepped away from the noise of the crowd, saw Sarah's name on her screen, and answered the call.

"Hey, what's up? I'm working."

There was a pause on the other end. An announcement over the hospital's PA system called for a doctor to the ER.

"Beck, Laura was brought into the hospital a few

minutes ago. She was left for dead at the side of the road near the Lakeshore."

Without hesitating, Becky said, "I'll be there as soon as I can."

She'd call Ellen on the way, tell her to send Kevin to cover the talks. He should have been doing it anyway if she hadn't interfered.

Already on her way back to her room to get her things, she fired off a quick text to Henry, letting him know to expect someone else. Laura needed her and she wasn't about to let her intern down.

The first flight she could get back from Ottawa landed Becky at Toronto's Billy Bishop Airport at 3:18 p.m. Since she'd had only carry-ons, she zipped through the airport, bypassing the luggage area, and found a taxi outside. Flights within the country were expensive, and she'd paid for it out of her own pocket, feeling no trace of guilt that the TV station would have to fork over airfare to send Kevin Moore to take her spot at the peace talks. Ellen had been sympathetic, though a bit annoyed at her early return. Becky knew her producer cared about Laura, and after the inconvenience of having to send someone else passed, Ellen would be mortified at her initial anger at Becky.

Sarah was waiting for her when she raced into the hospital's ER a half hour later. She rarely visited Sarah at work because they were all too busy doing their jobs and researching the apocalypse to engage in idle visits. The ER bustled with activity. Nurses ducking in and out of curtained off areas tending to patients. Doctors with sombre faces ducking in after them, emerging with no change in expression.

Sarah stood at the nurse's station, her stethoscope wrapped around her neck. The white lab coat with pockets in the front looked crisp, as if she'd just put it on. There was nothing about Sarah that indicated she was tired.

Since they were sisters, Sarah gave her a quick hug for appearances, took her hand, and walked down a corridor and to a bank of elevators.

"She's stable, so we put her in a room upstairs."

The elevator ride felt like the longest journey of her life. When the car jerked to a stop and the doors opened, Becky waited for Sarah to lead the way. They walked down a long corridor to the end of the hall. Sarah turned to the door on the right, pushed it open, and let Becky enter first.

The bright overhead lights made her squint until she became accustomed to them. It was a semi-private room with the first bed empty. Neatly made, it waited for a patient.

A blue curtain blocked her view of the other bed. She rushed into the room, stopping short when she saw Laura. With a bruised face, cuts on her lip, a gash on her cheek, machines hooked up to her monitored her vitals.

Sunshine from the window poured into the room, bathing Laura in a golden glow that highlighted her injuries. She looked frail, not anything like the strong, funny, accomplished person Becky knew.

Was this all her fault?

"What do we know about who did this to her?"

Sarah took Laura's wrist in her hand, shaking her head. "We don't know anything. Rachel is on it."

Becky's stomach bottomed out, a nauseous feeling overwhelming her. "Why is Rachel investigating?"

Finished taking Laura's pulse, Sarah gently placed her

patient's hand back on the bed. "It might end up being a homicide."

Numb, helplessness washed over her. "You said she was stable."

"She is, for now. Her injuries are severe. Whoever did this enjoyed beating her."

Becky trembled. Her hands shook. "We need to find out who did this."

"We will. The police think it was a mugging."

A horrible thought slammed into her head, that feeling of being responsible for this somehow. "She would have given them what they wanted."

Sarah rested a hand on Becky's arm. "I know. They're working on it."

A faint noise from beyond the curtain pulled Becky out of her thoughts.

A tall man with brown hair, sad eyes, and a rumpled shirt shuffled forward, carrying a cup of coffee. She recognized him from the pictures on Laura's desk. Her fiancé's face was haggard, his eyes red, hands shaking as he lifted the cup to his lips. He plunked himself into a chair beside the bed, staring at Laura. He gently took her hand and squeezed it.

"I'm so sorry, Mark."

He nodded, lips pursed. A tear slid down his cheek.

Becky pulled Sarah out of the room. "She is not going to die."

Sarah glanced into the room, then back at Becky. "We're doing all we can."

Becky shook her head. "You're not listening to me. She is not going to die. Either you do it, or I'll do it, but she is going to survive."

They'd done it once before. Healed someone when they first arrived, with injuries so severe it should have killed them. Sarah had been unable to stop herself from using what little power she'd had in order to save the beating victim. Now, they both had a lot more power.

"We can't. We don't know how much it will take."

Becky took a deep breath. "Laura has been helping me with everything when I started getting the tips. Maybe that's what prompted someone to attack her. To keep her quiet. To prevent me from finding out more. She will not die."

Sarah nodded. "I'll wait until her fiancé is gone. If she needs healing before that, I'll send him away somehow."

"Thank you." Becky dropped her shoulders with a deep sigh.

"Only enough so her body can take over. People will call it a miracle."

"That's what this world needs."

They returned to the room. Becky took a seat by the window and pulled out her laptop. Her gut told her Laura's attack was not a random mugging. She connected to the hospital's internet and pulled up her email to see if Laura had sent her anything that might have prompted the attack.

At the loft later that evening, the four of them sat in companionable silence after a dinner of garlic chicken and rice. Savoury scents from the dish still lingered in the air. Too tired after the long day, no one took care of the dinner dishes. They were piled in the sink, waiting to be cleaned or loaded into the dishwasher. Everyone's day had been exhausting with the effects of the apocalypse turning most events into serious incidents. Even Leah had drama at school dealing with more than a handful of bullies.

Students known for their understanding, caring, compassion, had turned bully on weaker students. For the first time since the school opened, there had been ten suspensions.

To chase away their blue mood, a comedy played on the television, but it was more background noise than actual entertainment. No one was paying attention to the shenanigans of the main character. They all sat in the living room, Rachel, Becky, and Sarah on the sofa, and Leah on the chair, but none of them even looked at the screen except when a cat came out to harass the main character.

Sarah shifted on the sofa and sighed. "Her fiancé finally left because visiting hours were over. I did my thing and Laura is going to make a full recovery. The worst of the damage is well on its way to healing."

Rachel turned to glare at Sarah. "We aren't supposed to use our power."

Becky's face flushed with heat. One of the reasons Rachel didn't want anyone else using their power was because she was jealous she didn't have more of her own.

Becky opened her mouth, but Sarah raised a hand to stop her comment.

"Funny that you mention that, again. I got some power back after healing Laura. I thought I would lose a lot of it. So no harm done."

Becky reached beside the sofa on the floor for her laptop. She pulled up her spreadsheet and entered the details of Sarah's power surge.

"When I have more time and I'm not totally distracted, I'll get Leah's help analyzing my spreadsheet to see why you got some power back."

She saved, then closed her spreadsheet. It should be easy, with Leah's help, to figure out why she was getting power back. The other angels would require more analysis or more data. She didn't have a lot of information for Rachel since she rarely got power back. Ditto for Leah. But Sarah had been able to get a few good power surges. Hopefully, there was enough to figure out a pattern.

Antsy, needing to do something physical for a change, Becky launched from the sofa and rushed to the kitchen. Her mind whirled with everything that had happened. She couldn't make sense of anything right now with Laura in the hospital. Every time she thought about the attack, a weight of guilt settled on her shoulders.

She opened the dishwasher and put the clean dishes away. Instead of loading it again, she turned the water on, reached through the stack of dishes in the sink, and put in the plug. She found the dishwashing soap under the counter since they rarely used it. Squirting a liberal amount into the quickly filling sink, she watched the bubbles form as the soap hit the spray of water.

When the water level was on the verge of overflowing, she turned the tap off. Plunging her hands into the sink, she enjoyed the sensation of the soapy water on her hands. The warmth of it seeped into her limbs, soothing her as thoughts about the investigation, the talks, the reapers whizzed through her mind.

She carefully washed each plate, rinsed it, then put it in the second sink. When they'd first created the loft with the magic they'd had left, she wondered why they would need a double sink. Until now, they'd never used both at the same time.

A tingle filtered through her wings.

The low, irritated growl from Rachel made Becky smile.

"You just got more power back."

She shouldn't smile. She felt sorry for Rachel. Out of

all of them, she had the least amount of power back despite her harping on the fact they needed power. Rachel barely had enough to cloak her wings.

"There is something good from today," Leah said. "I was able to find both the summoning and vanquishing spells for War. We just need the ingredients for each. The spells aren't the same. There are slight variations. Limestone from Mt. Hermon is on back order at the occult shop. We need that to vanquish him."

"Good job," Rachel said, successfully distracted from Becky's wings.

"Thanks. I also found a spell to turn the bullies into nice students again."

Rachel frowned. "Why would you use that?"

Leah shrugged and pulled a wing forward. "Kept the power I had and got rid of the bullying behaviour."

They couldn't put a spell on the entire planet to make people treat each other better. But with the newly found spells for War, a little hope seeped into her heart. She hoped it wasn't too late.

Chapter Thirteen

At the office the following morning, exhausted after a night of almost no sleep, Becky drained her coffee cup. She'd spent most of the night tossing and turning, thinking about Laura and why she was attacked. Not for one second did she believe it had been a mugging. Though chatter floated on the air and the chugging of the photocopier was the same, the office felt off without Laura there. She swallowed, attempting to dispel the lump in her throat. The area where all the interns sat was quiet today, everyone working silently, no one laughing.

Even if the police found out who had beaten Laura, would the law be able to do anything to them? War wouldn't get his own hands dirty, not for one person. Someone else had been responsible. An image of Conquest slammed into her brain. Beating Laura into submission was right up his alley and something he'd done before to gain control of the gang. It was too bad they didn't have enough power or ingredients to send both horsemen back to limbo.

Becky opened the last email the intern had sent her.

Last night, she hadn't been in her right mind to think about the contents after viewing it at the hospital. Now that she knew Laura would survive, she could focus, at least a little.

The email talked about weapons of mass destruction. Laura, following a route about what she thought the weapons text meant, ferreted out a few websites of interest for Becky to look at. She clicked on the first one that gave an overview of the weapons agreement Canada had made with other countries about their weapons.

The article mentioned that Canada had not officially had weapons of mass destruction, including nuclear and biological, since 1984. Becky leaned closer and scanned the rest of the article, which talked about the inspections she already knew about. Canada passed every year. As did every other country on the list of signatories. If they hadn't, there would have been news of the breach long ago.

Becky's gaze went back up to the key part of the article, at least for her. Canada had not officially had weapons of mass destruction. What about unofficially? Maybe politicians back then didn't want to give them all up, so they covered up their existence. But that would have required inspectors from the committee to be in on it. If the politicians, at least some of them, were reapers and the plan had been in motion for a long time, it was possible. Or maybe the fact that they wanted to hold on to weapons had nothing to do with the plan to bring about the apocalypse.

She continued clicking on the breadcrumbs of links in the article and finally ended up on a page about CFB Ralston. The same base her tipster had mentioned earlier when she wanted more information about their previous cryptic text about weapons. Maybe not just weapons, but weapons of mass destruction. Ralston was where the WMD would be if Canada did indeed have them. The inspections every year indicated everything there was disarmed. But she needed to get a look at the place.

Only one person could okay that trip for her.

She marched into Ellen's office, not bothering to knock since the door had been open. Her producer looked up, frowned, keyed something into her computer, then focused her attention on Becky.

"What can I do for you, Ms. Malak?"

"You can send me to Ralston."

"Any particular reason you want to go to Alberta?"

Becky quickly filled her in on the email from Laura that led her down the path to the base.

"No. We need you here."

"Kevin is covering the peace talks. Suzie can do my five o'clock spot for the news."

She didn't like the desperation in her voice, but she *was* desperate. She had to make Ellen see things her way.

"That email was the last thing Laura sent me before she was attacked. I have to follow it through."

"You think it has to do with why someone beat her?"

"Yes." It wasn't a complete lie. At least she didn't think so. The email could have been part of the reason someone had beaten Laura. War wanted them all distracted so he could do whatever he wanted.

Ellen sighed, dropped her chin to her chest, then looked up at Becky. "Okay. You've got a day."

"A day? I won't even be able to do anything until tomorrow morning even if I leave now."

"A day in the field. I'll give you some leeway with travel times. You need to finish your story on the gangs and do follow-ups on the earthquake. This little feature about the tips hasn't even been green-lit yet. You haven't sent me any notes or a pitch. Ready to tell me more?"

Becky bit her lip. "Not yet. I promise it will be good. I need more information, though, and this trip could help. I'll send something soon. I promise. I want all of my ducks in a row first."

Ellen turned her attention back to her computer. "I hope you find what you're looking for. I expect you back in the office Friday morning."

Becky nodded and raced back to her office. Ellen hadn't given her a lot of time. She pulled up a website with discount airfares, found a flight that flew non-stop to Calgary, and booked the ticket using her own credit card. More expenses that Ellen wasn't sure of wouldn't be a good idea.

Since she was only going to be there for a day, she didn't bother worrying about luggage. Almost everything she needed was in her purse or her computer bag. What she didn't have, she could pick up when she landed or ask for at the check-in desk for the hotel.

She fired off a group text to her sisters to let them know she wouldn't be home that night. Then she hurried down the aisles, pausing at Laura's empty cubicle for a moment, then continued out the door to the bank of elevators.

Though she was sure the base would be manned around the clock, by the time Becky landed in Calgary, the last thing she wanted to do was drive for two and a half hours, in the dark, in a province she'd never been to before. Instead, she found the nearest hotel she could, which happened to be the Calgary Airport Marriott. Since it was literally at the airport, she wouldn't have far to go when she checked out to go home. And she would be able to rent a car in the morning from the airport.

At the front desk, she waited for the clerk to check her in. She paid extra for the Wi-Fi, though she could have sat in the spacious lobby and logged on for free. When she received her key card, she requested to have some toiletries sent up.

On her way to the elevator, she grabbed a newspaper from a rack in the lobby and tucked it under her arm.

Once in her room, she flipped on the light, dropped her purse and laptop bag on the floor beside the king-sized bed, and collapsed onto the firm mattress. It felt like she'd been on the go for a week not two days.

Before she got too comfortable, she went to the mini fridge, grabbed a bottle of water, cracked the lid off, and took a long gulp. A knock at the door startled her. She checked the peephole. A uniformed hotel employee stood with a small bag dangling from her hand. Becky opened the door.

"The toiletries, miss."

"Thank you."

Becky held up a finger, indicating she wanted the employee to wait, then dashed over to her purse and pulled out a two-dollar coin. She handed it to the woman, who smiled, then hurried off.

Settling on the bed again, she thumbed through the paper to see if anything caught her attention. With the horsemen in Ontario, would any of the other provinces be showing the effects of them being on Earth? Nothing caught her attention, so she shoved the paper away.

She reached behind her to grab the remote for the TV from the bedside table. A clock radio displayed the time in bright red: 8:00 p.m. She turned the television on and channel surfed.

Since falling to Earth, this was the first time she'd be on her own for any length of time. At the loft, someone else was always there. And usually, it was all four of them. Rachel rarely had to be gone all night. And Sarah tried to be home every night even when she had a patient who needed a follow-up. She was getting better at letting other doctors help her. Leah, being a teacher, was home before all of them since she left the school at 4:30.

Channel surfing turned up a short snippet on the peace talks, indicating they were going well. Becky stared at the screen while the reporter from the local Calgary station spoke, trying to spot Henry and Kevin. The camera moved, panning left, to show people gathered in front of the ballroom chatting. War stood out like a rotten apple in a bag of oranges. There was nothing she could do about that. Whatever he was planning, she hoped it would take more time and wouldn't happen while the talks were going on.

Another segment showed people picketing in front of a hospital in Calgary. Omega signs decorated many of the protestors' signs. Becky sighed. The doomsday cult was probably everywhere.

She thought about ordering room service since it was available twenty-four seven. Though the clock now said 10:00 p.m., she was still on Toronto time and wasn't ready to go to bed yet. But she wasn't hungry and didn't want to waste food she probably wouldn't eat.

Instead, she found a channel that showed old movies. All of the ones listed were still new to her. They were after her time on Earth. *All* movies were after her time on Earth, and she hadn't had time to watch many since falling from Heaven. She settled on a romantic comedy from 1934 about a reporter and an heiress stuck together after the bus they were on left them behind at one of the stops.

She woke with a start hours later, to find another movie playing on the TV. Yawning, she picked up the remote and turned the television off. A quick glance at the clock told her it was 7:14 a.m. Though the curtains for the room were pulled closed, a thin sliver of sunlight spilled into the room. She didn't even remember falling asleep. It had been sometime after the couple from the bus hung up a sheet between them in the hotel room.

She rushed through a shower, then did the best she could with her hair after it was completely dry. The only makeup she had with her was what she carried in her purse. Since she wouldn't be on the air, she didn't bother with anything except foundation.

Ready to tackle the airport to rent a car, she sat on the bed first and called the office. When she showed up at the base, she needed to know who she would be asking for. The trip had been so last-minute she hadn't had time to find out.

After a few rings and no answer, she frowned and pulled the phone away from her ear to look at the screen to make sure she'd called the right number. A lump formed in her throat when she saw she'd called Laura's extension. About to end the call, she stayed her hand when someone picked up.

"CTBN, Dawn."

"Dawn, it's Becky Malak."

"What can I do for you, Ms. Malak?"

She liked that they didn't care for a lot of small talk. She didn't have time for that given her limited time in Calgary.

"I need to find out who oversees the weapons at CFB Ralston. I need to meet with them today."

"Do you want to hold, or should I call you back?"

"Call me back. As soon as you can, please. I'm headed to the airport to rent a car. It would be great if you had the name for me so I could go right to the base from there."

She ended the call, grabbed her purse and laptop bag, made sure she had her key card, then turned the doorknob hanger to Do Not Disturb before shutting the door behind her. She pulled it all the way forward to ensure it was closed, turned the knob to make sure it didn't open, then strode down the hall toward the elevator.

By the time she'd rented an economy car, Dawn called her back with the name of the person overseeing weapons at the base. Becky typed it into a note on her phone. She sat in the car, still in the rental place's lot, plugged her phone into the console, and pulled up the maps application. Once she'd finished punching in the street address of the base, a map, with a green line indicating her route, popped up on the screen.

She put the car in gear and drove off the lot. With the turn-by-turn directions on, she glanced at the map to see how long it would take her to get there. Two and a half hours if she went the speed limit.

By the time she got to the base, she was more than ready to get out of the car and stretch. All of her limbs, wings included, ached from being in the same position for so long. She pulled up to the security station, flashed her press badge, and waited for the guard to open the arm that barred vehicles from driving into the base unauthorized.

He frowned at her. "This is a military base, ma'am. I can't let you in. Contact our public relations office for a statement about our ongoing activities."

Behind her, another car had pulled up. Her only option was to pull through the U-turn area before the security arm and leave from the other side of the security station.

"Take a closer look at my badge." She held it up again, pointed a finger at him, and thought about being a high-ranking military officer who worked there.

Dazed for a moment, he stared even after she pulled the badge away. "Sorry about that, Colonel Malak."

The arm went up and she hit the gas before her magic wore off. If she lost any power due to her little trick, she would make it up to the rest of the angels later. Something was going on here and she needed to find out what.

She followed the street she was on until the end to what looked like the office building for the base. Other buildings lined the street and to the right, well past the decidedly military-looking structures, there was housing. She guessed there was also a school.

She pulled the car to a stop in a parking spot near the door. Would she have to use her power again? In order to not cause any problems, she thought about her supposed rank again, assigned it officially, if only temporarily, to herself. Military knowledge, missions, codes, and passwords flooded into her head. She looked at her press badge, which now showed her as Colonel Malak.

Satisfied the ruse would work for the hour or less she would be here, she got out of the car and took the stairs two at a time to the main door.

The guard on duty there held up a hand to stop her before she could go through the security turnstile.

"Ma'am, you can't go back there."

Panic raced through her. Had she already used all of her power? Rachel would kill her. But the information had poured into her brain like it had when they first set up their personas.

"I believe I can, Corporal."

She pulled out her badge and showed it to him.

His face flushed a deep red. "Sorry, Colonel." He

pressed a button and a green light on the turnstile panel appeared.

She pushed through the gate. At least she hadn't had to test whether her badge would unlock it. "I have a meeting with Major-General Hunt. Can you point me to his office?"

"End of the hallway on the left."

She nodded her thanks and forced herself not to rush. *Look like you belong and no one questions you.* Finally at the end of the hallway, she stopped in front of Major-General Hunt's door. Right across from his door was a double set of doors that required a pass card to get through. With no time for exploring, she knocked on the door.

A gruff, authoritative voice told her to come in.

She opened the door and smiled at the man sitting behind a large oak desk. He wore a standard officer's uniform. His salt and pepper hair was trimmed in a standard crew cut.

"What can I do for you, Colonel Malak?"

Relief rushed through her. She'd never tried a temporary persona before, and she didn't know how long it would last.

"I had a question about the inspections that the Biological and Chemical Defence Audit Committee does every year."

He folded his hands on top of his desk. "They all pass." He opened a drawer in his desk, pulled out a folder, and plunked it on his desk. "On the top page is the order to have the most recent weapons that were tested decommissioned."

She opened the folder and read the first page. "It says they're being moved to Ontario this Sunday."

"Yes, that's where they're decommissioned."

Further scrutiny of the document led to more questions. "Shouldn't it say on there that they're being decommissioned?"

Confusion crossed his face. He turned the sheet around. "It does."

It was her turn to be confused. "Where?"

He positioned the document so it faced her again. "Right here." A long finger pointed to a blank space on the form.

War. The horseman must have used magic so everyone who looked at the form saw what was supposed to be there. Her gaze focused on the destination of the weapons.

"Where in Ontario are they being moved to?"

A frown crossed his face. "CFB Kingston. It's right there on the form."

It was on the form, except it said Wavecrest for her. So that was what the construction was for. She was no engineer, but she suspected that the depth of the digging might have triggered the earthquake. Or it was a coincidence that the quake happened. But the quake itself did add another sign of the apocalypse to their growing list of events.

"Thanks for your time."

Before he could say anything else, ask her questions about why she wanted to know, she fled his office and walked as quickly as she dared down the hallway. There was a lot to chew on, but she could do that at home. She didn't want to be away from her sisters longer than she had to be. It seemed the centre of the apocalypse was Ontario, possibly Toronto specifically, and they needed to be together.

Safely in her car and on the road back to the hotel, she breathed a sigh of relief. She didn't stop checking her rearview mirror for anyone who might be in pursuit until she pulled into the car rental parking lot.

Chapter Fourteen

Early Thursday morning, the sun shone so brightly Becky wore her sunglasses to keep herself from squinting. The sky, a light powder blue, was dotted with a few white, fluffy clouds. A chill in the air forced her to zip up her coat right to her neckline. At least there was no snow on the ground. Temperatures had been above zero degrees Celsius for days.

She raced along the sidewalk on her way to Queen City Hospital, dodging the morning commuters who crowded the downtown core. When she reached her destination, she'd pick something up to eat in the cafeteria. Last night, she'd gotten home past 11:00 p.m. and been so tired she'd crashed into bed with her clothes on. Thankfully, her magic tricks at the base hadn't drained much of her power and she doubted Rachel would even notice the missing minuscule amount. But she hadn't stayed around long enough this morning to find out.

At the hospital, she took the elevator up to the fifth floor, raced down the hall, and paused outside Laura's room to catch her breath. Laura looked up when Becky entered, a faint smile on her face.

"Hey, how are you doing?" Becky took the seat by the bed Laura's fiancé had been using the last time she'd been here.

"I'm doing better. Still a little sore, but the doctors say I'm on the mend. Did you get the email I sent you?"

Becky nodded. "I got back from Alberta last night. I went to check it out."

"Did you find out anything?"

She scrutinized Laura's appearance. While the gash on her cheek had knitted together and the cuts on her lips were almost gone, she noticed the slight grimace every time Laura shifted in the bed.

"Not much, but enough for me to keep digging. Are you sure you're okay?"

"I'm fine. I promise." A muscle in her jaw twitched.

The hospital would give her what she needed to manage the pain, so Becky dropped that line of questioning. "How is Mark?"

"He spends all his time with me when he's not at work. He's trying to get a few days off, but his boss is being a jerk. They're busy with year-end and say they can't spare anyone."

The sound of the door opening drew Becky's attention to the curtain separating Laura's bed from the other one in the room.

Sarah popped her head around the curtain. "The nurses told me you were here. Can I talk to you in the hallway?"

Becky nodded. She put her purse on the floor, then followed Sarah to the hallway.

Sarah looked over her shoulder, then back at Becky. "We just received a notice saying the vaccine isn't as effective as initially stated and a new one will be sent to all drug stores, doctor's offices, hospitals, and clinics. To be given to people fifty-five and older first."

Her tipster had been right. How had they known before the hospitals? She guessed the delay in communication was because they'd still been working on the newest vaccine.

"Would you be able to get me a sample of the new one when it comes in? I want to have it analyzed."

"I will." She nodded to the door to Laura's room. "Don't stay too long. She had angelic help, but she still needs lots of rest to heal completely."

Sarah rushed off to check on patients. Becky returned to the room to find Laura reclined, eyes closed. When Becky grabbed her purse, Laura's eyes flew open.

"Sorry, I didn't mean to disturb you. I should go and let you get some rest. I'll be back later in the week."

"Okay. Thanks. I am a bit tired."

Becky left the hospital, opting for a breakfast sandwich at one of the family-owned coffee shops on the street instead of the cafeteria. Sarah loved the old building, but to Becky it smelled of death, bleach, and decay. As she bit into her sandwich, images of Laura's face raced through her mind. Would they find out who did that to her? Did she need police protection? If it had been a mugging, she was probably okay. If it had been more than that, her life might still be in danger.

Thankful she didn't have to go back to the TV station until tomorrow, and not yet ready to go home, Becky stopped in to see Rachel at work. She texted ahead so Rachel would be waiting for her when she came into the building.

When she entered the building, Rachel nodded at her and Becky silently followed her back to her desk before speaking. Other detectives in the unit were busy on phones or immersed in paperwork. Some were away from their desks, presumably at crime scenes or interviewing witnesses or suspects.

She pointed to Williams' empty desk. "Where's your partner?"

Rachel shook her head. "He took the day off to spend time with his family."

Rachel pointed to the chair beside her desk. Becky sank into it, taking a deep breath. Seeing Laura earlier fuelled her desire to find those responsible.

"What have you found out about Laura's attack?"

Avoiding Becky's gaze, Rachel took her seat. "It's not a homicide, so it is being handled by 50th Division." Before Becky could comment, Rachel held up a finger. "But I talked to a friend there."

Becky raised an eyebrow.

Rachel glared at her. "Yes, I have friends. Anyway, they have nothing at the moment. No clues. No witnesses. Even though the temperatures haven't been too cold, the guy must have been wearing gloves because there was no DNA either."

Becky slumped back in the chair like a petulant child who'd been told they couldn't have a treat before dinner. She crossed her arms over her chest and sighed. "It's been two days."

"I did take a peek at the CCTV footage and all of it in the area went out just before the attack happened."

"What do you mean went out?"

"In the gas station robberies we know Conquest orchestrated, all the footage went fuzzy right before anything happened. Same here. Everything working fine, then suddenly snow. Then the picture was clear again after the incident."

Becky sat up straighter. "War or Conquest must be behind it. But why? Laura's not an angel."

Rachel shrugged. "They had a reason. Maybe she was getting too close to information they didn't want you to have. Maybe they wanted to throw you off your game."

As much as she hated to admit it, Rachel might be on to something. If she was worried about her co-workers, she would be less focused on investigating the tips she'd received. She was sure they had to do with War now that weapons were involved. And it couldn't be a coincidence that reapers were in top positions in science, politics, and the military.

Did that mean Henry and Ellen were in danger too?

A detective, eyes wide, shock written all over her face, rushed over to Rachel's desk. "Detective Williams' house had a bomb thrown at it."

Rachel's face drained of colour. "Was he hurt?"

The detective shook her head. "He wasn't there. Took the family out for a day trip to The Toronto Zoo. Bomb squad is on the scene, checking it out."

Rachel picked up her phone and called a number. She tapped her foot on the floor as she muttered 'come on' several times. "Finally! Are you and your family okay?"

Becky glanced around the room, turning her back to Rachel and the conversation she was having with her partner. If she wanted to, she could use a little power on the phone so she could hear his side, but she afforded them some privacy. Rachel would tell her everything anyway.

After a few minutes, Rachel hung up.

"Does he have any idea who did it?"

Rachel frowned. "He said he didn't. But we both know it was probably one of the Grange gang."

"Was it? It can't be a coincidence that my co-worker was attacked. And now your partner has been targeted."

"You think this was War or Conquest."

"Don't you?"

Rachel sank into her chair. "I think you're right."

Rachel shivered for a second. She raised her eyebrows. Becky peeked at her sister's wings.

"Yes. A new small patch of white is there."

Becky made a note of it in her phone, to be added to the spreadsheet she was keeping.

"You know what this means?"

Becky nodded. "Sarah's and Leah's co-workers might be next."

She hoped they didn't go after patients or students. Ignoring the urge to visit Laura again, Becky left Rachel to her work and headed home. There was a lot she could do there, especially when they were all at the loft, to figure out what the tipster was trying to tell her.

***

Despite the worry gnawing at her stomach, aromas drifting into the living room from the kitchen made Becky's mouth water. They were all at the loft instead of the bar, with Sarah making dinner, because they needed the quiet to go over what she knew about the tips. With all of them working the problem, she hoped they'd be able to make sense of it all. She, Leah, and Rachel sat in the living room because Sarah shooed them away from the kitchen.

Muted, the twenty-four-hour news station on the television scrolled breaking news about the bomb that hit Detective Williams' house. Another headline reassured the viewer that the peace talks were still going well in Ottawa. After a few entertainment fluff headlines, a headline about the apocalypse scrolled by, with an interview with Father Ianetti playing above it. Hands shaking, Becky turned the television off.

"Dinner's ready!"

They took their places around the breakfast island. Sarah put a dish in front of each of them. Exotic spices teased Becky's nose. The red cabbage mixed in with the spiced beef gave the dish a splash of colour. Becky dug in with her fork, revealing the bed of grains the beef nestled on.

"What's this?"

"Farro. I went to St. Lawrence market and picked up some ancient grains." Sarah took a big bite of the dish, chewed, and swallowed. "It's delicious. Try it."

Skeptical, Becky took a tentative bite. A slight nutty flavour, with a hint of brown rice, exploded over her taste-buds. "It's good."

The others, seemingly satisfied that Becky had been the Guinea pig for the dish, dug into their meals.

Now that they were all together, Becky filled them in on what she'd learned in Alberta the day before.

"If Wavecrest was the location he was moving them to, he can't now because of the earthquake." She took a sip of her water.

Rachel finished chewing a bite of her dinner and swallowed. "But why do you see the truth and everyone else sees the lie?"

Becky shrugged. "Because I have enough power back to see it? All of us and probably the horsemen would see the truth. And they probably want a paper trail they can use to scapegoat someone when something goes wrong. And something will go wrong. What worries me are the last few tips dealing with the weapons and the rabbit hole that led me to."

She brought them up to speed on the committee that checked the weapons and biological agents at each base. The more she talked about it, the slower everyone ate, until their forks sat idle on their plates.

"You think he's going to release some sort of biological weapon?" Rachel asked.

The thought of it made Becky's stomach churn. With the horsemen involved, there was no telling what that agent would be. Would there be a cure for it? How could they stop them from releasing it?

"I don't know when, but yes." Becky picked up her fork again.

Rachel focused on Sarah. "We need to worry about your patients and co-workers." She turned her attention to Leah. "And your students and co-workers."

Sadness crossed Leah's face. "I heard about Detective Williams' house. I'm glad no one was there."

Rachel's jaw tightened. "They're trying to throw us off our game by hurting those we care about."

Becky raised her eyebrow. "You care about people?"

Rachel pressed her lips into a white slash. "Of course I do. I care what happens to him and his family. I don't want anything bad to happen to them because of me. Despite their flaws, most humans are inherently good. I'm at a loss as to how to keep him safe and still do my job as an angel."

Rachel's eyes widened. A shiver went through her, and she pulled a wing forward. A new white patch appeared near the tip. Becky pulled out her phone and made a quick note to add that information to the spreadsheet later.

Becky sighed. "We need to figure out War's plan for the weapons."

Her first thought was to get Laura to search for requested permits in small-towns near the border in Ontario. He'd be moving them somewhere else now. If they knew their destination, maybe they could expose the military for still having them. An image of Laura in her hospital bed flashed through her mind. Her throat tightened. One of the other interns would have to try to fill Laura's shoes tomorrow.

"If we send War back to limbo, do you think that will stop it?" Sarah asked.

Rachel shrugged. "It might slow it down. With him gone, the others would have to start over. If we send him back before Famine is summoned, it would give us a good shot at stopping the apocalypse." She turned to Leah. "Where are we with supplies?"

"I found a list of everything we'll require buried in some ancient texts. We have most of what we need to summon War and to send him back to limbo. We're waiting on a back order of limestone."

"Good. When it comes in, buy up all of it. That should hinder Father Ianetti's ability to summon War again."

Leah nodded. "Good idea."

It was a good idea, but if he already had a bunch in stock because he needed it for the others, Rachel's plan wouldn't slow him down at all. Now that they knew the ingredients to send War back, a glimmer of hope settled in her stomach despite the chance Father Ianetti had more limestone. The priest would mess up at some point. He had to. There was no way she was going to let anything happen to the people she'd grown to care about.

Chapter Fifteen

Oblivious to the stark beauty of the line of bare trees along Thirty Road, War snapped off the radio in his car, craning his neck back to ease the tension building there. On the road for an hour already, the drive to Smithville had been an errand he didn't have the time for, but it couldn't be avoided. Not as ideal as Wavecrest because it wasn't as close to the border, it was smaller in population, with more wide-open spaces. When the weapons arrived in Ontario, he needed to have a place for them.

He drove for another thirteen minutes until he hit the heart of the small-town. With only one motel, a family-owned, non-chain accommodation, he located the building easily. It had a square lobby, with an offshoot on either side with rooms all on the ground floor. The neon sign out front boasted free Wi-Fi, breakfast included for overnight stays, and a swimming pool. He parked in the small lot and marched to the main street, the centre of the town. Most of the population was concentrated near the main roads, but the outskirts, near the boundaries with neighbouring towns, had lots of unused land.

Town hall was located next to the library. A small stone building with crumbling stairs guarded on either side by a metal railing, the town hall appeared deserted. He took the stairs two at a time, pushed through the heavy wooden door, and stepped inside. The interior of the place was brightly lit, small, and smelled vaguely of burning wood. A fireplace on the right, in a waiting area blazed despite the above zero temperatures outside. Most of them would be headed someplace a lot warmer once the heart of the apocalypse hit.

With his fake paperwork in hand deeming a sizeable chunk of land to be military-owned, he marched up to a service window on the left to get the appropriate permits. Being a horseman with power, he could forgo all the formalities and start building anyway. But maintaining the ruse required power and focus he didn't want to spare. Things went more smoothly when it appeared everything was in order. Later, when the truth came out, people would see what had really happened. But by then it wouldn't matter. Besides, small-town folk wanted to make a buck and to bring work to their town.

Even with power, the paperwork for the permit took an hour with him waiting in one of the wooden chairs lining the left wall of the building. For a small-town, the office was bustling with folks coming and going, with all of the ten chairs occupied at one point. And that worked to his advantage as well. With a few whispered words here, a nudge there, he planted seeds of dissent in the town. A small, tight-knit community that would soon unravel with the rest of the province when his plan was in full motion.

When his number was called, he marched back up to the window, grabbed his permit, then headed outside to call the crew from Wavecrest. He already had them in place. They were ready to work. It made more sense than trying to find a crew in Smithville. He offered them the same bonus for getting the job done quickly.

The foreman accepted for himself and the rest of the crew. War went over the terms again to make sure the man understood everything.

He walked back to the hotel and got in his car. The build site was a twenty-minute drive from the centre of town. Meadows of brown grass as far as the eye could see. He tucked his phone under his ear as he exited the car. He waved a hand, and immediately a fence enclosed the area he needed for his bunker. A small building sat near the gate's entrance.

"Good. Get them here pronto. Everything is all ready for them to finish what has already been started." He waved his hand again to put in a hole deep enough for the bunker. Another wave of his hand added a digger and other equipment on the site. "Everything's here. The assembly needs to be finished."

Sleight of hand to set up the location was easy. It would take too much out of him to put in the bunker himself and affect the whole town's memory of it being built. Building the rest of it the hard way would take more time but leave him with enough strength to affect other things. Like the angels. He and Conquest needed to deal with them. The attacks on people close to them hadn't slowed them down much.

"I'll be there right away," the foreman said.

"Work through the nights if you have to. It needs to be finished by Sunday."

Something crashed on the other end of the phone, a mug possibly. "That's less than two days."

Gunther wiped a hand down his face. "The hole is

there, the permits are ready. All the materials are waiting. There's a huge bonus if you can do this on time."

If the foreman couldn't get it finished but did some of the hard work getting the hole deeper, poured the concrete, and started with the electrical stuff, Gunther could do a few waves of the hand to finish the job.

"It will be done," the foreman said.

Gunther didn't listen to much after that. After informing the foreman everything was ready and he would be going back to the city, Gunther ended the call, got back into his car, and started the engine.

Back on the road, he told the car to dial Conquest. The gangs needed to be riled up some more. And other people in the angels' circle needed to meet with some accidents.

Early Friday evening at the loft, the dishwasher whirring in the kitchen with their dinner dishes, Becky sat at the breakfast island with her laptop open. In the living room, Sarah, Leah, and Rachel sat on the sofa. The TV was tuned, as it usually was, to the twenty-four-hour news channel. When this was over, and she was back in Heaven, she would avoid news like the plague. It was so disheartening to see the events unfold. The stories about how horrible people were being to each other. The rise in violence. The increase in theft. The growing indifference.

At the bottom of the screen, the ticker proclaimed the peace talks to be going well. They'd been going on for a week and even though little progress had been made, some had, so that was cause for celebration, at least to her TV station. Above the ticker tape was a shot of the area outside the banquet rooms. The camera panned left and right. There was no sign of War, but he could have already caused damage and left to work on skirmishes somewhere else.

The news shifted to a story about getting the flu vaccine booster. A list of groups needing the booster urgently identified those prone to pneumonia, those who would be travelling, and those who were immunocompromised.

"Sarah, have you seen more than the usual number of people in the hospital for the flu?"

From the sofa, Sarah shook her head. "Not really. Not alarmingly so, though there has been a slight increase. It's nothing that is making alarm bells go off. The public health unit doesn't think it will significantly tax our resources."

"But there's still the recommendation to get the booster?"

Leah nodded. "They're having clinics on Monday at the school to get the students vaccinated properly."

"At the police station too," Rachel chimed in.

The list on the screen changed to one with reasons businesses should offer to vaccinate their employees.

"Do a lot of companies jump on board offering vaccines to their employees?" Becky pointed at the screen. She vaguely recalled receiving an email about it herself from the HR department at work.

Sarah nodded. "It cuts down on doctor's offices, pharmacies, clinics, and the hospital doing it. At least it did with the initial vaccine. I'm assuming the booster will be the same."

Becky's muscles tightened. Her pulse raced. "I'd like to know what exactly is in the booster that the original missed."

"I'm working on it." Sarah turned back to the TV.

Five chimes in a row drew Becky's attention back to

her computer and her email. Messages at the top from the interns were marked important.

She opened the first one and frowned. They'd found thousands of permits being requested, but they narrowed down the list by start time and found twenty that were now or within the next few days. There wasn't time to go to all of them.

The paperwork she'd looked at in Alberta came back to her. The date on the papers said the weapons were being moved on Sunday. Wherever the new place was, construction had to have started already. She dismissed the ones that were starting on Monday. And the few that had start dates on the weekend.

Satisfied for now that she had a manageable list, she created a quick spreadsheet to go over later. Now, she needed to determine when and why she and her sisters got power back. She opened her tracking spreadsheet. There should be enough data to analyze to find a trend with white returning to her wings.

"Leah, since you remember everything, would you mind helping me with the spreadsheet?"

"Sure." Leah pushed herself up from the sofa and sauntered into the kitchen. She sat on the stool next to Becky.

Becky finished putting in some of the data she'd noted in her phone. When she was done, she pushed the laptop toward Leah.

With a few clicks of the mouse, Leah added graphs, put in some filters, and sorted the data by angel. She pointed to the screen.

"You're missing some data here. The time you got a magical boost for getting burgers."

"That's right. Can you add it? Feel free to add anything else I forgot."

Leah filtered by angel to add in missing data. The uncivility of people affected Leah the most because of her photographic memory. It would be impossible for her to forget her second time here on Earth and the horrible ways people treated each other.

Leah leaned back, with the data showing all angels again, sorted by most power returned per action. "There's a definite pattern for you and for me."

Becky leaned closer to view the screen. Sarah and Rachel had left the sofa and hovered behind them, looking over their shoulders.

"What about us?" Rachel asked.

Becky shook her head. "You two don't have enough data yet." The look on Rachel's face sent a shiver through Becky. It wasn't her fault the eldest angel, by arrival time, and time being angelical, hadn't done much to get more white in her wings.

Becky filtered the data so only Leah's information populated the screen. "Look, every time Leah is happy with something, she gets a power boost."

"What about you?" Sarah asked.

Becky filtered the information again, so it showed only hers. "It looks like when I do things for myself, I get rewarded. When I delegate, I don't."

So simple, but she hadn't made the connection until seeing it in front of her. She pulled up her memory of the pawnshop owner getting shot. Even though she'd called for help, she hadn't actually done anything physical to assist the man. She could have tried to stop the bleeding, put a blanket around him to ward off shock, talked to him in soothing tones until paramedics arrived.

Now that she knew, she could do things on purpose to regain her power. A knot in the pit of her stomach told her she'd need all she could get very soon.

Sarah reached in between Leah and Becky to filter the data so it showed only her own. "This doesn't make sense then. Why do you get rewarded when you do something, but for me nothing happens? I'm only rewarded when I delegate. Your spreadsheet must be broken."

Becky unfiltered the information so all of the data appeared on the screen. "It's not broken. When you give leftovers to someone else, you're rewarded."

Rachel pointed to the screen. "And when you used power to save Laura, you got more back than you used."

Rachel flicked Becky's hand away from the mouse and grabbed it herself. She pulled up her information. "Mine makes no sense. There doesn't seem to be a pattern at all."

Becky nodded. "Not yet. It needs more data. We'll keep on it, don't worry. We'll figure it out."

Eager to test her theory, Becky went through actions she could take that would reward her. Would it work if she was consciously doing them? She had to believe it would.

"Why don't we go down to the basement and train?"

Becky turned on her stool in time to see Rachel's frown.

"It was a rough day at work. I'm not in the mood to train."

"That's okay. I can go alone. It won't be as effective since you're the expert when it comes to self-defence."

Rachel shifted from foot to foot, scowled at her, then nodded. "Fine. I'll go."

Leah jumped off her stool. "I'll go too."

They all looked at Sarah. "Sure, why not. I'll supervise."

Becky ducked into her bedroom to change into clothes

more suitable for Canadian s combat techniques and sword fighting.

When she came out, everyone was ready and the loft held the scent of freshly made popcorn. Becky took a deeper breath. With butter.

"I wanted something to munch on," Sarah said.

In the training room, Rachel flicked on the light, illuminating the equipment. On the far wall to the left, the swords and daggers gleamed.

Sarah walked to the back wall and took a seat on the bench, the bowl of popcorn in her lap. Leah joined her, dipping a hand into the bowl. Sarah frowned.

"You're going to eat that whole thing yourself?"

"I could."

Leah shook her head, tossed two pieces of popcorn into her mouth, then folded her hands in her lap.

"Pick your sword." Rachel nodded to the weapons on the wall.

Becky grabbed the heaviest one to increase her strength. Stamina was an issue as well, and after a few parries back and forth, she was usually out of breath. Rachel always gave her a reprieve. But War would not be so accommodating.

Rachel picked a lighter weapon. She wielded it expertly, legs slightly bent, hip width apart, waiting for Becky to attack.

The clang of metal against metal filled the training room. Sarah jumped at the first blow, from the noise.

After a few blows back and forth, the sword weighed a thousand pounds. Becky could barely hold it above her waist, ducking and dodging every time Rachel came near her. The whiz of Rachel's blade cutting through the air above Becky's head was too close for comfort. Big sister wasn't holding back, because War wouldn't hold back.

Becky sucked in a breath, willing her arms to move. She wanted to stop. Call it a night. But that's what she always did. Rachel was expecting her to give up again just as easily as every other time they trained.

Becky jumped back when Rachel lunged again. Though the weapons were dull, with protective plastic on the tips, a blow would still hurt. With the next attack, Becky ducked, then rolled across the floor. She took a deep breath, jumped up to her feet, and held her sword in front of her. Without missing a beat, she attacked Rachel.

Surprised, Rachel jumped back a second too late. The tip of the sword nicked her arm, drawing a line across the skin with the lead they put on the tips.

A tingle went through Becky's wings. She smiled.

From the bench, Leah clapped. "Congratulations! I'm so happy for you!"

Becky noted the little shiver Leah did, and her smile grew wider.

"That's not even fair," Rachel said. "She didn't even do anything." She pointed at Leah.

"We'll figure out yours when there's enough data." Becky raised her sword and turned back to Rachel. "Ready for another round?"

Rachel marched into the centre of the room, raised her sword, and waited for Becky to follow. They exchanged blows until they were both exhausted. More lines from the lead tips marred Rachel's skin than Becky's.

Huffing and puffing three hours later, Rachel and Becky lowered their weapons and returned them to the wall. Sarah was already back upstairs, tapped out from observing them an hour earlier. And Leah stretched out on the bench, almost asleep.

Becky nudged the youngest angel. "We're going back upstairs."

Leah jumped to her feet, stretched, and yawned. "You've improved a lot since training first started."

Becky smiled as she trudged up the stairs. She had to get a lot better if she was going to defeat War and send him back to limbo.

Chapter Sixteen

Late Friday evening, Gunther sat behind his desk at the armoury, finishing off a large order of fries after having eaten the burger that accompanied it in three bites. He'd been starving. Now that he was corporeal, he often forgot he needed sustenance in order to function properly.

The door to his office was locked. MerlinCrackers, the hacker he'd used before, sat in one of the chairs opposite him, fingers flying over the keys of his laptop. This was the most secure place they could meet to do business in person. When the young hacker arrived, Gunther had effected a glamour so MerlinCrackers appeared to be a fellow officer visiting him. He could have easily messed with the cameras instead, obscuring the young man's face, but glitches in the surveillance would draw attention he didn't want right now.

For the purposes of tonight's test, the office would suffice. Later, he and Conquest would need to make their apartment more secure. Once Famine and Death arrived, his office would not be large enough for all of them to gather to go over plans.

Merlin's eyebrows drew together as his fingers paused over the keyboard. The incessant clacking of keys stopped, and the room was silent for a moment. Then he smiled, nodded, and the clacking returned.

"Fry?"

Gunther shook the container and held it in Merlin's direction.

"No, man. Can't stop. You gave me a time limit."

Gunther nodded. He checked his watch. The hacker had less than a minute to complete his task. It was imperative that the hacker follow the directions precisely. Any deviation would render him useless and Gunther would need to find someone else to help. He didn't have time to find and break in another hacker. In this one instance, he was rooting for the man to succeed.

Five seconds before the timer ended, Merlin let out a whoosh of breath and leaned back in his chair.

"Done."

"You're sure?"

He turned the laptop around, showing a small fortune now sitting in an offshore account belonging to a high-ranking U.S. government official.

"And it's untraceable?" Gunther prodded.

Merlin nodded. "Exactly as you asked."

"Excellent. I have another task for you."

Merlin turned the computer around, hands poised over the keyboard, waiting for instructions.

"Shoot."

"What kind of damage can you do to the stock market?"

"A lot. You want all of them to tank? Only a few?"

"Start with the Japanese and the U.S. markets for now."

"You got it. It won't be all that noticeable until

Monday when the markets open again. Well, Sunday night for the Japanese market."

Gunther nodded. "True. But what a surprise it will be. Make it look like foreign manipulation from Russia if you can."

Merlin cracked his knuckles and started working. After an hour of repeated attempts to break into the markets, Merlin let out a sigh. "Finally."

Gunther leaned back in his chair to think up other tests for the hacker. All the tests helped his cause, moved his plan forward, and convinced him MerlinCrackers was the right hacker for the job.

Half an hour later, Merlin stopped typing. "Done."

"Good. How are you with hacking into social media accounts? Running ads?"

"I could do it with one hand tied behind my back."

"Good. I need you to hack into several social media ad accounts and run targeted ads to U.S. people about the need to defend one's way of life. Carefully, though, so the ads aren't tagged as violations. I'm going to get a drink from the vending machine. Do you want anything?"

"Something with a lot of caffeine."

Gunther stepped out of the office, thankful for the opportunity to stretch his legs, and locked the door behind him. He was War. He wanted to be on the ground, commanding armies. He didn't care which human side. But this was how he would get there. Convincing opposing sides that war was the only solution.

He put coins in the vending machine, the plink of them falling echoing in the empty hallway. For himself, he opted for a refreshing lemon lime pop. For Merlin, he selected an energy drink that promised the consumer five hours of increased focus and vitamin C.

When he returned to his office, Merlin sat with his

hands at his sides, the laptop teetering on the edge of Gunther's desk.

"Problem?" Gunther handed the drink to Merlin.

"No. Finished. It wasn't hard to tweak the ads they already had going, change the copy, and redirect to a different website."

Impressed, Gunther refrained from showering Merlin with too much praise. Instead, he took his seat, opened his beverage, then took a sip.

"You've done well. I'll need you back on Sunday for something bigger."

Gunther clicked his mouse button, which had been hovering over a submit button. "Check your account."

Merlin pulled his computer back onto his lap. "That's a large sum."

"There's more where that came from if Sunday is successful."

Merlin nodded and packed up his equipment into the backpack on the floor by his chair. He slung the bag over his shoulder. "See you Sunday."

Alone in the office again, Gunther finished his drink. His hands itched for combat. His skin tingled for conflict. War was so close he could almost feel the pain of radiation peeling the skin from his body.

<hr>

Still sore from training the night before, Becky reclined on the sofa, soft pillows cradling her back. She lay there, slightly vertical, facing the TV and the window behind it. No matter how much her muscles protested, she would return to the training room, continue her workouts, until she was satisfied War wouldn't kill her with his first blow.

Leah sat on the chair beside her, absently scrolling

through information on her laptop. At least Becky assumed that's what she was doing. The youngest angel had been silent for over an hour, gaze glued to the screen while Sarah and Rachel sat at the breakfast island in the kitchen.

"Since we have an almost complete list of things we need for War, I'll go to the shops and pick up what I can." Rachel jumped off her stool.

"I'll go!" Becky groaned as she moved her legs, sliding them over the edge of the sofa.

She stood, her muscles screaming at her to sit again. The pinched expression on Rachel's face made it look like the angel had sucked on a lemon. Rachel's long fingers tapped against the island.

"Leah can come with me so I don't forget anything."

Rachel opened her mouth, probably to protest, but closed it again. "Fine."

Leah jumped out of her chair. "I'll get my coat and purse."

Outside, the temperature hovered above zero, making the air crisp, but not so cold that she wanted to retreat again to the warmth of the loft. Becky and Leah walked down Queen Street, dodging the weekend warriors who didn't let a little thing like the weather get in their way of shopping. Slightly less crowded than during the week, the downtown core still thrummed with activity.

The shop was packed. Inside, it was warm, helped in part by the candles that flickered in each corner of the store when the door opened. The scent of jasmine and lavender teased her nose, calmed her spirit.

Customers murmured to each other, pausing when Becky and Leah entered, then returning to their conversation. Celtic music played, not so loud that people had to raise their voices, but loud enough to soothe, allowing the customer to sway to the sounds.

Becky picked up a shopping basket from a stack of them beside the door while Leah surged ahead in search of the items they needed. Five minutes later, arms full, Leah returned, dropping herbs, candles, incense, and crystals into the basket.

"There are a few other things I saw. Back in a jiffy."

Leah disappeared into the crowd again. Becky slowly made her way to the counter, hoping by the time she arrived, Leah would have returned with the remaining items.

At the counter, Becky hoisted the basket up and plunked it down beside a display of crystals. Leah arrived with the last of the items.

The clerk, a young woman with blue hair, looked up and smiled. "Did you find everything you need?"

Leah shook her head. "Actually, I couldn't find the limestone from Mt. Hermon."

The woman nodded. "Popular item these days. It's still on back order."

As the woman began to ring in their purchase, Becky leaned forward. "Has anyone else come in here looking for these things?" She waved her hand over the counter.

"A few weeks ago."

Leah did a little dance on the spot. "What else did they pick up?"

If Father Ianetti was the customer, and they had no reason to think he wasn't, finding out what else he bought would help them piece together the spell ingredients faster for the other horsemen.

The clerk shrugged. "I don't want to say. That's personal for them."

Becky pulled out her press pass. "It's for a story. We won't say what they bought or who bought it. But it will help a lot with the background for the piece. We could even feature your store."

The woman gazed at Leah, then at Becky again. She huffed out a breath. "They also picked up saffron, mandrake, and dodder."

She finished ringing up their purchase, dropping it all into a reusable canvas bag.

Outside, Becky took a deep breath of the cool air. The shop, with the candles and customers, had been too warm for an extended stay.

"Those other things she mentioned could be for Famine," Becky said.

"Or Death. We still don't have a complete list of what's needed to summon him."

"True. Some of Conquest's and War's items overlap."

The mention of War sent a chill down Becky's spine, colder than the air outside. Despite her misgivings, she didn't have a choice. With Conquest imprinted to Rachel, and Becky with the most angelic energy, not to mention the sword training, it made sense she would be the one to fight him. At least she was stronger now than she'd been weeks ago, giving her a better chance of not being fatally injured.

Chapter Seventeen

R einvigorated by the walk to the store and the fresh air, Becky sat at the breakfast island, laptop open. She'd thought about going into the office when she and Leah had returned from the shop because Sarah had left for the hospital shortly after they'd gone. But the office wasn't the same without Laura and she didn't want to be at the office on a Saturday without her.

Becky scrolled through social media posts, taking note of the ones that talked about hackers leaking information. It was the usual scares, millions of email and password combinations compromised. A hospital in England plagued with ransomware until they paid a fee to unlock their data. Supposed military briefs discussing an incursion planned for Russia. Underlying all of that were the rumours that the U.S. dollar was falling and investors worried about what the stock markets would look like on Monday.

Becky travelled down the rabbit hole of links, checking Snopes to see what was true and what wasn't. Nothing had been confirmed yet for any of it. An ad popped up in her feed about buying local, defending a proper way of life. She clicked to dismiss the ad.

She opened a new search window and typed in hacker. Suggestions for hackerrank, hacker typer, hacker news, and ethical hacker popped up in the search bar. She selected ethical hacker and read a few of the articles the search engine returned.

With a little angel mojo, she zapped the forum, giving herself street cred and a long history of posting. Roaming the forum, she found a hacker who looked to be popular and knowledgeable. She posted in a newbie thread, asking if anyone could answer questions for her.

In another window, she continued to scroll through social media. Posts clogged her feed from people complaining about seeing a lot more ads than usual. And for things they weren't interested in. Ads about prepping and needing to arm themselves when nothing in their preferences indicated they would be interested in those topics.

On the forum, her private mailbox pinged. Becky switched to that and clicked to find a message from Ladyhacker.

LADYHACKER: Hey. Saw your post. I can try to help.

INVESTIGALHACK: Thanks. Have you heard anything about someone hacking into places to leak information?

LADYHACKER: :) Well, sure. All the time. That's not what we do here though.

INVESTIGALHACK: Of course not. But you've heard of other hackers doing that? The ransomware in England for that hospital?

LADYHACKER: Ya. Heard about that. People have been complaining on social media lately too, that the site took money for ads they said they never set up.

INVESTIGALHACK: Could a hacker do that? Break into someone's ad account and change their ads?

LADYHACKER: Sure. A hacker can also make information look like it's coming from one place when it's actually coming from somewhere else. But we don't do that here.

INVESTIGALHACK: Thanks. Would it be possible to get in touch again if I have more questions?

LADYHACKER: Feel free. But we won't help you do anything illegal.

After reassuring the woman that she had no ill intentions, Becky signed off from the hacker forum. Her mind wandered back to the story about the U.S. being up to something in those briefs that were leaked. Though she believed military information would be harder to crack, and she wanted to believe it was all a hoax, the churning in her gut told her it was true.

She fired off emails to U.S. government agencies, as many as she could find email addresses for, warning them about the possible threat. She listed her credentials, giving her personal and business phone numbers. If they didn't even realize they'd been hacked, they couldn't do anything to stop the leaking information. Was it too late? What if they wouldn't listen to her? She was a reporter from Canada. What would she know about the military operations they had going on? Just like tips to the TV station, they would have to vet her information before taking action and by then it might be too late.

Tapping her fingers on the breakfast island, Becky gazed around the loft, looking for something to do. She needed activity. Movement. She couldn't sit still waiting for someone to get back to her. It would drive her blood pressure through the roof. She rotated on her stool and her gaze settled on the sink. The dishes from dinner last night and breakfast that morning were already done. Even the dishwasher sat empty because Leah had put the dishes away before joining Becky at the shop.

It was too early to start dinner. Lunch was usually a free for all. None of them ate the same thing for the midday meal. Rachel usually skipped it. Leah had something small when she was home. Sarah had something that would have worked as a dinner. And she usually opted for something simple. But, with the ominous hacker activity, her stomach rebelled at anything more solid than water.

Tempted to scroll through more social media posts, knowing they would only serve to fuel the acid in her stomach, she closed the lid of her laptop. Maybe she should take up playing video games. People seemed to lose themselves in those, forgetting their troubles for a short time.

Though she wanted to do something, there wasn't much to do until the final ingredient came in to summon and send back War. They already had a list of things needed for Famine and a partial list for Death. If they worked every waking moment on stopping the apocalypse, they'd burn out. So they tried to have downtime.

It was even too early for a trip to Baron's. The music didn't start until after seven.

A jingle of keys from the doorway snagged her attention. She turned to see Sarah walk through the door. Exhaustion marred her face. Her wings, cloaked for anyone not an angel, drooped forward as if in defeat. No new white patches were apparent.

"Rough few hours?" Becky asked.

Sarah nodded. "It's getting overcrowded from the victims of violence." She fished something out of the pocket of her coat. "I managed to get this for you."

Becky took the vial and examined it, noting the name of the flu virus strain on the label. "The booster?"

"Yes. We've only given out a few at the hospital, but other places might have given out a lot more."

"Thanks."

Becky grabbed her phone and called Dr. Karimi. After a brief conversation, she grabbed her coat, depositing the vial in the right-hand pocket.

"I'm dropping this off with Dr. Karimi. I'll be back before dinner."

Sarah nodded. She shuffled over to the sofa and dropped onto the cushions. "I'll let the others know."

Excited to have something to do, Becky raced along the sidewalk, relieved Dr. Karimi had no problem going into work on the weekend.

At the lab, he greeted her with a smile, ushered her into his office, and shut the door. He wasn't the only one there on a Saturday. Lab workers stood at stations, carefully examining vials of fluid, preparing slides, putting them under microscopes.

She handed over the vial without preamble. "I'd like this to be analyzed. But not by Dr. Althaus. Someone else."

He raised an eyebrow but nodded. "Well, there's Dr. Brad Hunter. Dr. Liz Morris, and Dr. Simon Adams."

She pulled up pictures of the three suggestions on her phone and turned the device around to show him the screen. He pointed to a picture in the middle.

"That one is hard to make out. They're blurry."

"What about the other two?"

"Their pictures look fine."

She did another search, eliminating Dr. Morris. With her fingers, she pinched the screen to zoom in. Dr. Hunter had a tattoo peeking out from the short-sleeved shirt he was wearing. The bottom of it looked like the one she'd seen on the doomsday cult members' signs on the picketing line in Calgary.

"Dr. Adams. Please send it to him for analysis. Can you get back to me once they've checked the vaccine?"

"Of course. I don't suppose you can tell me what's going on?"

She frowned. "I can't say yet. But it's not good."

In the training room after lunch, Becky stretched her muscles to loosen them for the workout to come. The frenzy of activity and speculation online left a knot in her stomach. Something was coming, soon, and they had to be ready for it.

Rachel waited for her to finish limbering up, standing against the wall, arms crossed over her chest. Leah and Sarah sat on the bench to supervise after finishing a workout of their own. Though Becky was the most likely to confront War, they all needed to be ready to take up a sword, dagger, or other weapons to fight.

Sufficiently warmed up, Becky marched over to the weapons on the wall and retrieved her sword. Today it was a little lighter than she remembered, which was a good sign.

Rachel breezed past her and picked a larger sword that weighed less. It was more unwieldy due to its length, but easier to lift.

Before Becky could return to the centre of the room, Rachel lunged. Instinct kicked in and Becky raised her sword to block. She manoeuvred them away from the wall and danced around Rachel, waiting for the angel's next move.

They parried back and forth, the sound of metal clanging against metal filling the room. Becky smiled, dropped her sword slightly while she danced away, and crooked all of her fingers back and forth, urging Rachel to attack.

Rachel sneered. "You're not taking this seriously."

Becky raised her sword. "I am."

"You don't have a killer instinct yet."

The thought of killing someone horrified her, but this was War they were talking about. A horseman. Who wouldn't even die, just go back to limbo, waiting for the next apocalypse.

"I'll do better."

From the bench, Sarah sighed. "I'll fix it."

With a flick of Sarah's finger, Rachel morphed into War. Becky, startled, jumped back, immediately raising the sword in front of her.

"Sarah!" Rachel frowned, but with War's face, the look was comical.

Becky took a defensive stance, never taking her eyes off her opponent.

"Oh, I think I feel a tingle in my wings!" Sarah said.

Leah clapped. "I see a new patch of white. Beck, I'll remind you later to mark it down in the spreadsheet."

Rachel moved forward, towering over Becky now that she looked like War. Becky moved back, her heart racing. A sneer crossed Rachel's face and she lowered the sword. Becky raised her sword to block. The force of the attack made Becky's arms shake.

She jumped back, watching Rachel's every move, trying to anticipate when the next blow would come.

After an hour of training, Becky's legs and arms felt like jelly. She could barely lift the sword, but she forced herself to keep going.

"We're training with swords because War uses a sword. But how are the balances Famine carries going to be a weapon?"

Rachel, still looking like War, shrugged. "Maybe it won't be, exactly."

The voice of War in their training room felt like an intrusion. A violation of their security. Until Sarah turned the glamour off, War would be among them.

Leah huffed. "It's not fair that Death has a sword and beasts. We'll all need to fight him."

Rachel attacked again, this time from the left. Becky turned her upper body in that direction and blocked the blow. A rush of air forced out of her lungs with the exertion. She bent over, shaking her head.

"I'm tapping out."

Leah jumped up from the bench and ran to the swords on the wall. "My turn!"

Sarah waved her finger and the image of War turned back into Rachel.

"Thanks. I didn't like looking like him." Rachel turned her attention to Becky. "If we can get War in close quarters, you'll do great with the sword."

Doubt crept into her mind, but she nodded. She hoped Rachel was right. They needed to slow the priest down and knock the rest of the doomsday cult down a notch or two. One of the best ways to do that was to send War back to limbo before he could do too much damage.

Chapter Eighteen

U nable to read one more conspiracy theory, Becky paced the living room Sunday afternoon like a caged lion ready to dart into the hallway as soon as the door opened. Sunlight streamed in through the windows, warming the floor. Sarah padded around the kitchen, making an inventory of what they had, what they needed grocery-wise. Rachel sat on the sofa with the TV turned on, but the sound turned down. And Leah perched on the chair, working on her laptop.

"We're running low on a few things." Sarah held up a list as she walked into the living room.

Becky stopped mid-step and spun around to face Sarah, who now sat on the sofa in the corner closest to the TV. "I can pick up groceries."

Rachel frowned.

"We'll figure out yours."

"I'll go with you. Looks like a nice day out." Leah closed her laptop. "I can research day trips for my students later."

The walk to the grocery store was short. When they'd

first arrived, if a convenience wasn't nearby, they rearranged the neighbourhood to accommodate. Once they'd figured out their purpose on Earth, they wanted as many stores, hangouts, work places within walking distance as they could get. They hadn't been able to relocate the school where Leah worked, but that wasn't far by bus.

The doors of the grocery swooshed open. A security guard stood inside the doors, scrutinizing people as they entered. He was over six feet tall, well built, with a face that broached no trouble. The black uniform he wore belonged to one of the many security services Toronto offered. This one had a white symbol on the arm.

"You're new," Becky said.

"Yes, ma'am. A lot of stealing going on lately. Some violent customers." He flashed them a smile. "I'm not going to have to worry about you two, am I?"

"We'll be good," Becky said.

They started with the produce section because it was the first set of aisles once you entered the store. As they proceeded to go up and down the aisles, dropping things into their cart, Becky noted how many items on the list were not being crossed off. The all-purpose flour, sugar, and yeast were out of stock. She grabbed whole wheat flour instead. A pack of sugar cubes.

"What's going on?" Leah asked when they reached another aisle that was supposed to have bottles of water.

"There's a storm coming. People are stocking up just in case."

With the warm weather they'd been having, she and many others in the city had forgotten that it was actually winter. She hadn't been following the weather on her station for a few weeks now. But had seen a sound bite about the approaching storm yesterday.

With a little over half the items on the list, they checked out and hurried back to the loft.

Sarah frowned as she pulled the groceries out of the paper bags. "I can work with this stuff."

Invigorated after the walk, Becky grabbed her laptop from the coffee table, sat on the sofa, and thought about what to do next. Email. She checked her inbox, but there were no new messages from any of the people she'd tried to get in touch with.

Discouraged but refusing to give up, she pulled out her phone and made some calls. Each one left her disappointed. No one was taking her concerns seriously. It wasn't like she could tell them she had divine knowledge that something was about to happen. She would sound like Father Ianetti and the rest of the doomsday cult.

She punched in Kevin Moore's phone number. They'd listen to him. All she had to do was convince him to take action. After they stopped the apocalypse, she was going to fix things and give him his anchor position back.

Kevin answered right away. "Becky, what can I do for you?"

She filled him in on her research, the hacker information, the leaked documents, her attempts to alert someone in the U.S. government.

"I don't know what else to do."

He sighed. "You've done all you can. Presented the case. It's up to the people to act. Look, I believe you, but it's hard to make people listen to something they don't want to believe."

They chatted for a while longer, then she ended the call. Rachel was also hanging up from a call.

"I have to go into the office. Four homicide cases just came in. The weekend team is swamped." She retrieved her gun and badge from her room, threw on her coat and pulled the loft door open. "I'll try to be back by dinner, but no promises."

"We'll save you a plate," Leah said.

Pinging noises from Becky's laptop drew her attention away from Rachel's departure. Message after message popped into her inbox with subject lines about the violence in the streets. The four homicides Rachel had mentioned. Gang violence on the rise. Road rage out of control.

She scanned the list until she came to a different subject line, from one of the interns at work, about hackers. Becky opened the message. Ladyhacker had helped them find out more information about the leaked documents and other security breaches. Another hacker, one excellent at what he did, only left tracks on purpose. A sick feeling churned her stomach. She read further.

There were tracks from the documents, the rumours about the U.S. being up to something.

The tracks led back to the White House.

***

Despite the roiling of her stomach, Becky finished her dinner, leaving nothing on the plate. She sat at the breakfast island, facing the living room, Sarah beside her. Rachel, back from a few hours at the station, and Leah across from them. The meal itself was delicious with the right amount of savoury garlic, with a touch of sweetness from the mango. It was Ladyhacker's message about the trail leading back to the White House that nagged at her. Set her stomach churning with the implications for the world.

Her phone buzzed. She picked it up and read the message before it disappeared from the screen. Heart racing, she flicked a finger at the TV. The television blared to life, still on the twenty-four-hour news station.

Rachel's face reddened. "Becky!"

Before she could explain, Rachel's phone buzzed. Sarah's pinged next. Then Leah's.

Becky nodded to the TV and pointed at the screen. Dizziness overwhelmed her. Her hands shook.

Solemn news reporters relayed the information that a missile had struck Russia. Specifically, St. Petersburg.

Rachel banged her fist on the island. Leah gasped. Sarah dropped her fork.

Heart racing, denial coursing through her body, Becky rushed to the living room, picked up the remote, and turned the volume up on the television. Still holding her phone, she jumped on social media. Memes of World War III blew up her feed. Calming voices in the storm demanded proof, urging the public not to jump to conclusions. Reminding people of the alerts in the past, including the scare in Hawaii that proved to be a false alarm.

Though she wanted to believe those wise voices urging scepticism, the knot in her stomach told her it was true.

"Details are sketchy at the moment," Kevin Moore proclaimed from the newsroom. "We are waiting for confirmation from Russia that a bomb has detonated in St. Petersburg. It is unknown at this time if this was a terrorist attack."

Knees weak, Becky sank onto the sofa cushions. She racked her brain for instances of terrorist attacks on Russian soil. They weren't uncommon, but the most recent one she could remember happened years ago. From the information flashing on the screen, this wasn't a home-made bomb with low yield.

She ignored the text messages and opened the phone

app on her device. Her producer answered on the first ring.

"Is it true? Some influencers on social media are saying it didn't happen. Others are saying not only it didn't happen, but that it's a hoax."

Ellen's heavy sigh crushed Becky's heart. "All the information we have so far says it's true. Something hit Russia. They're trying to determine what, and where from."

"Is it possible it was a meteor? They've had large impacts there before."

"I suppose anything is possible. We've got people in Russia and we're trying to get in contact with them. Communication has been wonky since the strike. Your other pieces will have to be put on hold. I want all you can give me on this attack by tomorrow morning."

Not reassured, Becky thanked her producer for the information, promised to be ready at any moment to go into the office, then ended the call. A lead ball formed in the pit of her stomach. She knew where Russia would say the object came from. And she knew what it would be.

On the television now was a split screen showing the U.S. president and the Canadian prime minister admonishing the actions. So, the governments knew or strongly suspected it was a bomb.

The sound on the U.S. president went silent, the split screen dissolved into one, the camera focused on the prime minister.

"We have already been in touch with Russian leaders to offer aid. In this difficult time, our thoughts are with the Russian people."

He continued with his prepared remarks, then took questions. She lowered the volume. No matter how simple or complex the question, he never truly answered any of them when it came to terrorist acts. Inevitably reporters would ask if it was terrorism, and what would be done in the future to make sure it didn't happen again. If her instincts were right, the Earth was charging fast into having no future.

The scroll across the bottom of the screen proclaimed breaking news. Early indications showed the object, confirmed as a bomb, came from the United States.

The scene cut to the president, the prime minister's sound muted.

"The White House will get to the bottom of this tragedy and help Russia in any way we can."

He stepped away from the podium, shutting out questions, and entered the White House.

Determined, Becky sat up straighter, pulled in a deep breath, and grabbed her laptop, which was sitting on the coffee table with the lid half closed. She opened it and pulled up the hacker forum. Thankfully, since she'd already used her angelic gift to get her in, she didn't have to jump through any hoops to prove she belonged there. She clicked on her messages and pulled up the thread with Ladyhacker.

INVESTIGALHACK: Can you find out anything about the bomb hitting Russia?

LADYHACKER: Give me a few hours.

INVESTIGALHACK: Okay. Ping me as soon as you have something.

She had until Monday to work on the story. Horrific scenarios careened through her mind, but until she had more information, she needed to think positively. It was obviously a mistake. If there had in fact been a bomb, it had been fired by accident. The United States would smooth things over. Everyone would be frenemies again.

"This is a joke, right? A hoax?" The hopeful tone in Leah's voice broke Becky's heart.

"I'm waiting to hear back from someone."

Unable to sit still without refreshing her browser every five seconds, Becky launched herself off the sofa and paced the room in front of the window. A soft glow surrounded the streetlights. It was still mild out. All the snow was gone. She peered down at the empty street, an image of destruction flashing in her mind.

A few minutes before eleven, her laptop pinged.

She ran back to the sofa.

LADYHACKER: Two bombs were fired. They were made to look like they came from the United States. The hacker didn't leave much of a trail. I can't tell yet where they actually came from. He tricked the bombs into thinking they had the official launch codes.

INVESTIGALHACK: Thanks. Please keep digging and let me know if you find anything else.

She signed off with the chat and leaned back against the cushions.

"What did she say?" Rachel asked.

"It's not good. It was made to look like the U.S. fired on Russia."

Leah's face paled. "Why hasn't Russia retaliated already? With their surveillance, they would have fired back as soon as they saw the bomb coming."

Rachel shrugged. "Maybe War had a hand in that. We know the horsemen can disrupt surveillance. Maybe he did. And they didn't see it coming."

Sarah nodded. "Maybe he's still interfering and not letting Russia retaliate."

Becky shook her head. "But why? He's War. He wants a war, so why stop this one from happening? Especially if, as I suspect, he had a hand in that bomb hitting Russia."

"He might have another agenda that would be worse," Rachel said.

Sarah had changed the channel on the television to a more robust news channel, one of the CTBN affiliate stations for the city. Behind the news anchor, pictures of devastation from Russia filled the screen. Smoking piles of rubble that were once buildings in Moscow and Saint Petersburg. People running in horror, faces streaked with tears and dirt. A death toll flashed on the screen and they all gasped. Over 70,000 fatalities, with more than double that for injuries.

The shot changed to the doomsday clock. Changed from 100 seconds to midnight, it was now midnight.

With the increase in uncertainty in the world, Father Ianetti had added midnight masses to the church's schedule. He ushered the last of his lingering flock out the door, shaking their hands, nodding politely as they praised him for his words. Once the last person had left, he locked the door.

Walking through the nave, he checked each pew for missals not properly stored in the pocket of the pew in front. When he saw those, he paused, put the book where it should be, then continued until he reached the front of the church.

Unable to put off the inevitable any longer, he rushed to the office for a quick check to make sure everyone had left for the night. Then he raced to the rectory and his small set of rooms to gather what he needed. The summonings were necessary, but each one took a little more out of him than the last.

He carefully laid out the black robe, black pillar candles, the pewter bowl, holy basil, his athame, ancient grains, and salt. A quick run through of the checklist in his head told him one item was missing. He went to his cupboard and pulled out the sigils he'd created on parchment for each of the horsemen. After having to summon War again, he'd made extra copies of each sigil just in case. He pulled out the one for Famine and put it on the bed with the rest of the items.

He undressed, folding his clothes neatly and placing them on the trunk at the foot of the bed. He took a deep breath and shuffled into the bathroom where his salted bath waited. Bracing himself for the cool water, he squared his shoulders, then plunged in. Inch by inch was torture. He preferred to get the shock out of the way all at once.

Cool water cascaded over him as he settled in the deep tub. The gritty salt rubbed against his thighs, keeping him in the moment, unable to get completely comfortable. Anxious to get the ritual started, he rushed through the bath, lingering only long enough to be sure he was fully cleansed.

He pulled the plug in the tub, got out, and grabbed the old, rough towel from the rack beside the bathtub. Slightly more absorbent than a paper towel, the towel left areas of his body still damp even after a second rub down.

He returned to his room, donned the robe, gathered the items in a burlap sack, then raced through the hall of the church to the back garden.

The air was cool, quiet, and still, but not uncomfortable. A few stars twinkled in the night sky. A stone altar set inside a circle of rope waited for him. No one ever ventured into the garden, except that one time, especially in winter, so he had the circle and altar ready at all times. Before starting the ceremony, he dropped the bag on the ground and went to the gate to make sure it was locked. Even though he was guaranteed seclusion, he had been caught off guard once. But he had done the ritual early, too soon after an evening mass. With it being after midnight, he was confident he would remain alone.

He returned to the altar and set up the candles. He placed the small dagger, his athame, on the ground in front of the stone. On top of the stone, he placed the pewter bowl, with all the items save for the sigil, inside.

He fished a lighter out of the robe's pockets, then disrobed. The air chilled his already cool skin and he shivered. He lit the candles, raised his arms, and recited an incantation to call on the four corners of the Earth. When he was satisfied that his circle was sealed, he lifted the athame, pricked his finger with the tip, and squeezed five drops of blood into the bowl. He lit the sigil, dropping the paper in as well. A small spark of fire crackled and the scent of burning grain filled the air.

He rushed through the summoning incantation, muttering it over and over again in Latin, calling on Satan to answer his plea. As had happened before, the fire gave way to smoke. The air didn't move. For minutes nothing happened. Then, the sound of horse hooves, thundering toward him, filled the air. A wisp of smoke coalesced into the shape of a horse that ran past him.

Out of the lingering smoke, a form took shape. Tall, with black hair, Famine materialized before him. Father Ianetti could count his ribs. Sharp hip bones jutted out from his body. On one pencil-thin arm, there was a tattoo of a balance scale.

"Location and month?"

Startled by the horseman's booming voice, Father Ianetti jumped. "Toronto, Canada. It's January."

Clothes formed over Famine's body. First shoes with a thick sole, followed by jeans, a long-sleeved shirt, and finally a light coat.

"War and Conquest are—"

"I can sense them. Thanks for the invitation."

With more energy than he should have given his appearance, Famine jumped over the gate, disappearing into the night.

Chapter Nineteen

Early Monday morning, the buzz from Becky's phone pulled her out of a fitful sleep. Filled with dreams about countries crashing into the sea, the world cracking apart to drift into space, the dreams were so vivid, so real, her heart tore into a million pieces. Even if they couldn't stop the apocalypse, the planet would go on. And that broke her heart even more. What was Earth without people?

She grabbed the phone and swiped to answer the call. "Becky here."

"We need you in early." Ellen's voice was clipped, no-nonsense. It sounded like she'd been up for hours.

"How early?"

"Now. It's all hands on deck. We've got interns looking into the bombs. There's a press conference later this morning outside City Hall."

After assuring her producer she would be in soon, Becky breezed through her morning routine in half the time it usually took her. Adrenaline pumping, she rushed into the kitchen, thankful to see a fresh pot of coffee waiting for her. Empty dishes in the sink told her she was the last one up. She gulped down a cup of caffeine and put her mug in the sink with the rest of the dishes.

Sarah, Leah, and Rachel sat in the living room with the television on, glued to their spots, watching the continuous news footage. More pictures of a devastated Russia filled the screen. And a scroll across the bottom said that both parties at the peace talks in Ottawa walked away from the table. Had her sisters even gone to bed? She'd been first to drag herself away from the news, knowing today would be a long day.

"I'm headed to work now."

Sarah shook her head as if she'd been in a daze. "Already?"

Rachel pried herself away from the television, stalking over to the breakfast island and sitting facing the kitchen instead of the living room. "I should get ready for work too. Today is going to be...different."

"Everything will be different now," Becky said.

She grabbed her purse and laptop, checked to make sure she had her pass for work, then left.

The early morning, fewer commuters, and increased speed due to the caffeine rush helped to get her at her desk in record time, ready for what the day had to throw at her. She dumped her things on her desk, then rushed to Ellen's office.

Kevin Moore was already there looking fresh, in a crisp dress shirt paired with a navy blue suit. She took the only seat left, the one beside the door.

Ellen sighed and crossed her arms over her chest. "I need you and Kevin down at City Hall for the statement from the mayor, police chief, and Major-General Fertig. Get Henry. Make sure he brings a backup camera."

Becky straightened in her chair. "The major-general is going to be there?"

"Yes. Now get a move on. The news doesn't wait for anyone."

Becky and Kevin bolted from their chairs and hurried through the maze of cubicles back to their shared office. Before she could pick up the phone to call her cameraman, he appeared at the door to her office.

"Ready?" he asked, shooting a glance at her and Kevin.

By the time they arrived at City Hall, the police already had a section of the pavement behind the Toronto sign cordoned off. A podium had been set up with an array of microphones attached already from the various news channels. The reporters on scene sat on benches beside the sign, waiting for the press conference to start.

At precisely 8:00 a.m., the police chief stood behind the podium to address the gathered crowd.

"Yesterday an unprecedented event occurred that may cause citizens to panic and act out. We want to make it clear that this conflict is not a reason to start looting. The city will go on as normal. The country will go on as normal. After your questions, Major-General Gunther Fertig will have a statement."

Only two reporters had questions for the chief, as everyone was waiting to hear what the military had to say about the situation.

When War took his position behind the podium, Becky's heart pounded. More than anything, she wanted to send him back to limbo. Convinced he had something to do with the bombs, she wondered what he would say.

He gazed over the crowd and cleared his throat. "Thank you for being here this morning. The Canadian military condemns the actions of the U.S. government." He looked directly at her. "Reliable sources confirmed the United States deliberately fired two bombs at Russia last night, killing more than 90,000 people and injuring 200,000."

Her heart twisted. The fatalities had gone up overnight. The slight grin on his face when he looked at her vanished a second later. She looked around. It didn't appear anyone else had noticed. Was he taunting her? There was no doubt in her mind that he'd done this. Somehow fired bombs and made it look like the United States had done it. Was that why he'd been moving weapons closer to the border?

He took questions from the reporters, but Becky wasn't listening. She had to contact Ladyhacker again and see if there was a way they could prove a hacker was involved. She was sure nothing would lead back to War, but something had to lead back to a hacker.

When the news conference ended, she hurried back to the TV station with Henry and Kevin. It had been fourteen hours since the bombing. She hoped Russia waited before doing anything drastic. They had to be using independent sources to confirm what was all over social media. Maybe the hacker wasn't as good as Ladyhacker said he was. There was a chance he'd slipped up and Russia would discover the mistake. Realize the United States had nothing to do with the bombs.

She sat at her desk and stared blankly at the empty page, the cursor flashing, mocking her. Ellen would want a story. They needed copy for the midday news. And for the five o'clock news. Kevin would do an amazing job with his story for the late-night news.

Gasps from the cubicles pulled her out of her chair. Interns, the receptionist, the weather team stood, shocked looks on their faces. Some of them had tears streaming down their faces. Becky's stomach hollowed out. Her knees threatened to lock. She moved slowly into the main area of the floor.

Ellen burst out of her office, eyes red, face flushed. "News just came in that Russia retaliated. Three bombs hit the U.S. a few minutes ago. They hit California, Iowa, and Illinois." She pointed at Becky and Kevin. "Get to makeup. You're doing a spot now."

After a whirlwind of getting prepped for the camera, Becky sat behind the anchor desk, Kevin on her right. The cameraman counted her down, and she waited for the red light to come on. She plastered a sombre expression on her face and looked directly at the camera.

"It appears war has effectively been declared. We have received confirmation that Russia has fired bombs at the United States."

Kevin took over, but she didn't hear him. Leah would be able to tell her the significance of targeting those three states. They had been picked for a reason.

Shock rippled through the station the entire day. By the time Becky wrapped her day and got home, it was well past dinner. Kevin would be going on-air for the eleven o'clock news. The loft was quiet. The sink still full of dishes, which now included that night's dinner plates. Foregoing food, she crawled into bed, determined to come up with a plan in the morning.

Famine parked his black hybrid sedan in front of a weathered building behind a white SUV and red muscle car. Now that he was settled into a life he created for himself, it was time to discuss the next steps with his fellow horsemen. He turned the car off and the heat blasting from the vents immediately died. Pulling his coat tighter around his emaciated frame, he got out of the car.

Cracked concrete stones formed a pathway leading to the front door of the apartment building. He heaved the door open, welcoming the warmth of the lobby as a wave of hot air hit him. The light over the sofa in a waiting area to his left was burnt out. A guard, sitting behind a desk on the right, smiled. A name tag on the right top pocket read Gary.

"Can I help you with something?"

Famine waved a hand in the air. The guard nodded as if remembering something. He turned his attention away from Famine, yanked open the door of the mini fridge behind the desk, and reached inside. A freezer bag clearly marked Betty sat in his palm. He ripped it open, pulled out the sandwich, and took a huge bite.

Famine smiled. Whoever Betty was, she would go hungry unless she arrived before the guard could finish eating everything in the fridge.

The elevators were old and rickety. Clanging, groaning sounds filled the area once he pressed the call button.

War's floor was immaculate. Dark red walls made the hallway appear like it was closing in on you. Halfway down the corridor, a bright light illuminated the door to War's abode, welcoming guests. Famine rapped on it three times in quick succession.

War swung the door open and stepped aside so Famine could enter. The interior was spacious, with a large living room in the centre, flanked on one side by a wall with two doorways. One leading to a kitchen area and one to a dining area. The other wall served as a leaning spot for the sofa, a couple of end tables, and a bookcase. At the far end of the living room, there was a door leading to a hallway where Famine assumed the bedroom and bathroom resided.

"Nice place."

War ushered him into the dining room where Conquest sat facing the door.

"'Bout time you got here." Conquest nodded to a chair opposite him. "Have a seat."

Famine pulled the chair out and settled onto the soft cushion. "I'd like some food."

War grumbled something inaudible but stomped to the kitchen. He returned with chips, nuts, and drinks. "If you want something else, we'll have to order in."

A hunger pain cramped Famine's stomach. "This should do." He grabbed a handful of chips.

"What name are you going by this time?" Conquest asked.

"Zach."

"He's Vic, and I'm Gunther. What can you tell us about the priest? When will he be reuniting Death with the reapers?"

Zach finished munching a mouthful of nuts. "Not for a while. Summoning me wiped him out." He glanced around the room and peered into the kitchen, craning over in his seat. "Do we all live here now? Last time we were all here, we weren't all in the same city."

Gunther frowned. "Not ideal, but fine. In the meantime, we have work to do. Russia and the United States are fighting, but we need more. Countries along the Russian border will be in more conflict soon. And yes. This will be our base of operations and a place to crash while we're here."

"Have steps been taken to ensure pestilence?" Zach opened a pop and guzzled the sugary liquid, finishing with a satisfied smack of his lips.

Gunther nodded. "It started rolling out a few days ago."

Vic leaned forward. "Gang wars will be reignited in the city soon."

Gunther pointed at Zach. "You need to take care of the food chain. The conflict with Russia should help with scarcity, but you need to boost that."

He nodded. It had been decades since he'd been here last and he was looking forward to the new varieties of food the Earth had now. Food that wouldn't last long. With the war Gunther had started, and the conflicts yet to come, food would be in short supply. Zach would turn that food insecurity into a food scarcity.

"Good." Gunther smiled. "Once Death gets here, we can lay waste to the place and the planet can start over."

Zach's stomach growled. "In the meantime, can we order a pizza?"

Chapter Twenty

Unable to sleep, Becky sat in her office at the TV station early Tuesday morning, drinking her second cup of coffee. The interns slumped over their desks, seemingly at the station all night. The news never stopped, and the station reflected that with people bustling about at all times of the day and night. But it was a little quieter outside the normal nine-to-five hours of usual business. She savoured the relative calmness while it lasted. As soon as the rest of the staff arrived, the calm would shatter, nerves would fray, tempers would flare.

Becky poked around her email, barely paying attention to the subject lines. It felt like none of them mattered anymore. The only thing that mattered was getting the world to see that they'd been manipulated. That two countries had been tricked into starting a war with each other. A war the entire world knew no one could win.

Frustrated, she hopped onto the hacker forum and sent a private message to Ladyhacker, requesting more information on the bombs. Everything she could find to help prove a hacker was responsible. According to data Russia analyzed, the bombs had been fired from Montana. News agencies around the world reported found documents saying the weapons were hidden there in breach of several accords.

While she waited, Becky read urgent emails, marking the rest to a follow-up folder she would check later. Her mind refused to focus on the trivial items that still wanted attention, despite the conflict between Russia and the United States.

After finishing a third cup of coffee, replying to most of her email, and writing out the copy for her dinner broadcast, her inbox on the hacker forum showed a red dot.

She clicked the message, skimmed the contents, then printed it as well as the attachments Ladyhacker had sent. Wishing for something stronger than coffee, she gathered the papers and marched to Ellen's office.

"It wasn't either country's fault." Becky dropped the papers in the middle of Ellen's cluttered desk.

Her producer picked them up, her brow furrowing deeper with each page she read. "Go ahead with a story, but tread lightly. We're in the middle of two countries with enough weapons to wipe us out too. Probably enough weapons to wipe out half the planet. We'll put you on midday. You've got two hours."

Stomach churning on her way back to her office, Becky racked her brain on how to proceed. Her attempts to reach out to U.S. officials had proven fruitless before. But now that she had some documentation, maybe someone would listen to her.

She picked up the phone and called every number she could in an attempt to get someone from the president's staff on the phone. When that didn't work, everyone told her the president and his staff were too busy, she composed an email and attached everything, along with her analysis and that of Ladyhacker, keeping the woman anonymous. She hit send and repeated the same steps for Russia.

Trying to get a hold of anyone in Russia was difficult. Communications were down in areas where the bombs hit. She hoped the email reached someone who could talk sense into the country's leader.

With the emails sent, she worked on her story. Everything she knew went into the copy. During the broadcast, she pleaded for reasonable voices to prevail. Someone in either staff had to see the truth of the events, how they'd been manipulated to put two superpowers to war against each other. The trickle effect wasn't good either. Smaller nations were invading other nations. Fighting along borders ensued where once they had tenuous peace.

When the red light above the camera winked out, she took a deep breath. Everyone in the studio came up to congratulate her on the research, saying it might give the two nations pause.

Back in her office, stomach still roiling, she forwarded everything to the police. All the information Ladyhacker had given her pointed to the hacker being in Ontario. That didn't surprise her. War would have been able to meet with him, point him in the direction to start a war.

She called Rachel and asked her to vouch for her with the cyber-crimes unit so they would take action sooner.

"For this, of course I will." There wasn't a hint of disdain in Rachel's voice.

"Thanks. I'll be home for dinner, but I might be a little late."

Now that the special broadcast was over, she needed to focus on her dinner newscast. Somehow she would find a way to mention the hacker angle there too.

She went through the rest of the day waiting for her phone to ring, or an email to come through from an official from either country. She missed Laura. Though she was mostly healed, the hospital was keeping her to make sure she was completely out of danger.

The evening news flew by, Becky reading it off the teleprompter without processing the information until she came to the end and squeezed in a bit about the hacker. She looked directly in the camera, pleading with viewers to keep an open mind.

"That was a great broadcast," Ellen said. "I hope they listen to you."

Becky unclipped her microphone and retreated to her office to gather her things. After a sad day of increasing casualties, she speed walked to the loft. It was a home away from home and helped her focus her thoughts.

Dinner was ready by the time she arrived. She plopped down on a stool at the breakfast island, facing the living room. The TV was on, scrolling news like it did most days when they were home. Sarah's face, haggard from a long day, made her look a decade older than she'd been when she died and became an angel. Worry lines around Rachel's eyes marred her smooth skin. Even Leah looked worn out, her eyes sunken.

"Long day?" Becky asked.

They all nodded.

Leah took a sip of her water. "I was trying to calm my students all day. They're all worried."

"They should be," Rachel said. "Unrest in the streets is hitting an all-time high. Patrols are busier than they've ever been. Homicides have been going up. I expect more of the same."

When the prime minister appeared on the television, Becky hopped off her stool, dashed to the living room, picked up the remote, and raised the volume. Returning to her seat, she placed the remote on the island beside her plate.

"I want to remind the Canadian people that this conflict is not with us. Rest assured that we have defence missiles ready if any armaments are headed for Canadian soil. You are safe. With new credible information that a hacker is responsible, the United Alliance of Countries is reaching out to both sides to encourage them to talk things out."

"Do you think they'll listen?" Sarah asked.

Becky shrugged. "I hope so."

She finished her dinner, not tasting it. Dread settled in the pit of her stomach, worrying about the days and weeks to come. The longer it took for them to send War back, the worse things would get.

Wednesday morning, Becky was in the office before the start of her usual workday so she could catch up on emails and follow-up with communications sent to politicians who might be able to help with convincing the presidents of both countries to talk to each other. More messages had arrived in her inbox overnight on the hacker forum.

Ladyhacker, seemingly up all night, had sent dozens of documents and files with data. The data was a foreign language to her, but the documents from CFB Ralston should be useful. She needed to know what the documents said to the average person before she forwarded the information to the authorities. Even in electronic form, they indicated the weapons were headed for Wavecrest.

Kevin ambled into the office, plunked his half empty

coffee cup on the desk, and sank into his chair. He looked as shell-shocked as everyone else.

"Hey, take a look at these." Becky turned her laptop around so Kevin could roll his chair over.

His eyes widened as he read. "You mean we still had weapons we weren't supposed to have? Why send them to Kingston now?"

Becky shrugged. "Trying to get rid of them before more people found out. Members of a doomsday cult have insinuated themselves into all aspects of society. I think they kept the weapons secret so they could do this."

Kevin leaned back in his chair. "You think *we* fired on Russia?"

"I think the doomsday cult is responsible, with the help of the hacker. But yes, I think it was Canadian members of the cult."

"You think the hacker is part of the cult?"

Becky shook her head. "I'm sure he was paid enough, though."

"Paid enough to possibly die in the aftermath of a war he started?"

"Maybe he was promised a spot in one of the luxury bunkers the morning show has been going on about."

The morning show and twenty-four-hour news station, in short segments midday, had been reporting on luxury bunkers some of the city's wealthy had purchased years ago. The price of admission was high, but they had all the amenities and plenty of food, water, and medicine to last for years.

"They're pretty exclusive. It would have been a good incentive. You sending that stuff to law enforcement?"

"Of course."

When her phone rang, she held up a finger to pause the conversation. She picked up the receiver and listened to Rachel's news that the hacker was in custody. She hung up with a sigh. That piece of good news wouldn't make a difference if the United States and Russia decided to annihilate each other.

"They've arrested the hacker. He was trying to hack into security for one of those bunkers. Cyber-crimes picked him up twenty minutes ago."

"Maybe that's what they promised him. He could have a spot, but he had to hack in and add himself to the authorized people."

The more she thought about it, the more Kevin's hypothesis made sense. At least if they felt any qualms about outright lying to the guy. Somehow, she didn't think War cared as long as the job was done. But maybe it had been an incentive to get the war started faster.

At 5:00 p.m., she went on the air and rattled off the usual news stories that all felt less important now with the threat hanging over their heads.

"We do have some good news tonight. The hacker responsible for firing the bombs and masking their trajectory so it appeared they came from the United States has been caught."

Images of the devastation in the U.S. and Russia cycled on the screen behind her. It was early days, but speculation of food insecurity due to the places the bombs landed in the U.S. had resulted in hoarding of staple items in northern states and some parts of Canada.

"Stay tuned for more breaking news on the ongoing crisis. And Kevin Moore will be on tonight with your local news."

She signed off and sprang out of her chair. It wasn't a crisis. It was War. And the longer the horseman was here, the worse things would get. If Russia and the United States managed to smooth things over and no more bombs flew through the sky between the countries, another conflict would erupt somewhere else.

On her way down in the elevator, Sarah called to tell her the item that had been on back order was in.

Lightness returned to her chest. "I'll pick it up on my way home."

Chapter Twenty-One

With a lightness in her steps she hadn't had in weeks, Becky yanked open the door to the occult shop on College Street. It was a few hours before closing time and the place was packed. Most customers lingered in the crystals aisle, probably looking for protection crystals. A few dawdled in the herbs aisle. Though the herbs sold at the store were mostly for spells, healing, and protection, some doubled as cooking herbs. In a pinch, you could pick up what you needed for a recipe if the grocery store was out of what you needed. Tonight, though, she suspected everyone was looking for some form of protection against what was to come.

Despite the peace talks crumbling, there was hope they could slow the deterioration of society if they could send War back now. Accusations from both countries of conspiring with the United States or Russia sent all the delegates away from the table. Now that the limestone from Mt. Hermon was in, they could take action.

Hands trembling, she gathered all the holy basil she could hold, because they would need it to summon Famine as well. At the check-out, she asked the clerk about the limestone.

The woman, a long black braid draped over her shoulder, reached under the counter. "Here it is. Sorry it took so long to come in. The limestone is hard to get."

"I'll take all you have that isn't already spoken for."

The woman's eyes widened. "Hoping to work a lot of magic?"

"Something like that."

"I can give you all but one."

Becky nodded and the woman rang up the sale. Purchases in hand, she rushed back to the loft.

The place was empty. She did a quick search of the cupboard where they'd decided to keep all of the summoning equipment and ingredients. Everything for summoning War and sending him back was gone. They were already upstairs waiting for her.

Not wanting to lose any more time, she ran up the stairs to the roof. The door was propped open so they could get back down again after they were done.

Making sure she didn't move the brick holding the door slightly ajar, she stalked over the threshold.

When the door settled back into place, making a soft noise, Rachel spun around. "Finally! Are you ready?"

Becky nodded.

An altar was already laid out, the pentagram and candles in place. Inside the circle was a small dagger. Outside the circle, a sword waited for her. It was the heaviest of the swords she'd been training with.

Becky stepped inside the pentagram while the others stood nearby. It would take three of them to distract War enough for Becky to get close to him.

When Rachel nodded, Becky lit the candles, added all the ingredients to the pewter bowl, then pricked the tip of her finger. She waited until the drops of blood mixed with the herbs and metal in the bowl, then she lit the sigil on fire and dropped the paper to join everything else.

They all chanted the incantation to summon War.

Five minutes ticked by. Her heart beat faster. Should they try the incantation again? Had they missed something? Panic raced through her body. If they missed something to summon him, they might forget something needed to send him back. Fighting Conquest had bruised their pride. They'd thought it would be simple. A few words, a few ingredients, and poof. But the horseman was stronger than they'd anticipated. It took over a week for Rachel to recover completely.

A wisp of red smoke appeared in the air. The pungent scent of horses wafted across the rooftop. Hoof beats sounded. Far away at first, then louder, as if right on top of them.

War materialized. A muscle in his jaw twitched.

"I was in the middle of something."

Becky hunched down and grabbed the sword. She swung it at him, hoping to hit a vital organ, but missed. He jumped back, arching out of the way.

A sword materialized in his hand. A wicked grin turned up his lips.

"Very well."

He thrust his sword forward. Becky dodged.

Behind her, Rachel, Sarah, and Leah emptied the bowl and tossed in the new ingredients.

She had to keep him busy long enough for them to get everything ready. She sliced through the air, aiming for War's waist. With a flick of his hand, his sword came down to block her.

He backed up and took a swing at her. Becky charged forward, sword out in front of her perpendicular to the ground. Running him through would barely slow him down, but it might move him back enough for them to start the vanquishing spell.

He was faster. He danced out of the way, a smile crossing his face. With a grunt, he hefted his sword above his head and brought it down full force. She raised her arm, blocking the blow with the bottom third of the sword, close to the hilt.

Summoning every ounce of strength she possessed, she shoved upward and outward, pushing the sword away and War backward.

"Now!" Becky yelled.

Leah hurried over, flicked a lighter open, and touched the rooftop. A ring of fire encircled War.

Rage turned his face red. "You can't stop us. When Death comes, the Earth is doomed."

"So Famine is here. Thanks for that."

Becky charged again, pushing War close to the circle's edge. A sizzling sound split the air. He howled in pain and pulled himself back.

"It's fueled by holy oil."

Leah raced back to the others.

Now that he was trapped within the flames, the others focused on mixing what they needed. Becky circled War, thrusting the sword tip forward. She nicked his arm, which only angered him more.

He growled. Tossed his sword on the ground and charged at her, head down. Heat from the fire prevented her from backing up. She had no idea how it would affect her, but she hoped she had enough power back to protect her. She dodged right, but he anticipated her move and compensated. His shoulder plowed into her stomach, knocking her to the ground. Her sword flew out of her hand, clattering in the holy fire.

A heavy fist landed blows on her face. The sound of her cheekbone cracking sent chills down her spine. Pain exploded in her face.

Gathering her strength, she pushed him off and rolled out of his way.

Moaning, she reached for her sword, hesitant, bracing herself for the heat. She waited until the whole sword was blazing, then gripped the weapon. The handle remained cool to the touch.

Standing, she realized he had his sword in hand again.

He charged forward. The weapon entered her stomach and kept going. When he pulled it out of her, she crumpled to the ground.

"No!" Sarah's voice sounded far away.

Before Becky's eyes fluttered closed, she saw War approach the wall of fire that separated him from her sisters. The scent of burning flesh mixed with sulphur assaulted her nose. Sizzling skin suddenly stopped cooking.

She forced her eyes to stay open. War was gauging the fire. Searching for gaps in the flame where he might slip through with minimal pain and damage.

She sucked in a breath and coughed when her breath hitched. Digging deep, she summoned her angelic gifts to mend the hole in her stomach.

Reaching out a hand, she pulled War away from the ring of fire with her power. She knew how to get it back. If she survived.

War turned toward her, eyes flashing. "Good little angels should stay down."

"Even when I was alive, I wasn't a good little anything."

She pushed herself up. Took another breath that didn't hurt this time. A pool of blood on the ground reminded her how vulnerable they all were.

Inching away from the slick puddle, she kept her eyes focused on War. Willing him to watch her. The longer she gave her sisters to finish preparing the ingredients, the better.

He raised his sword. Jutted forward. The tip nicked her arm before she could parry. Healing herself was causing her reflexes to slow down.

Too close to her, he raised his sword and heaved it down. She blocked it again. This time her arm trembled from the exertion. Tapping into every reserve she had, she grunted, screamed, pushed upward with her sword.

He stumbled backward.

Her sisters were chanting now. She forced the sounds of their voices out of her head. Focused on War.

She surged forward. Sliced his waist. He howled in pain and leaned over.

"You're not going to be able to stop what's happening. Even if you send me back, my brothers are here. And Death will be stronger."

"We will stop it."

They circled each other, sizing each other up. Though he'd been injured, he didn't appear to be any weaker.

"The sacrifices of the many will benefit the few that are left," he taunted.

She lunged forward. The tip of her sword penetrated his stomach. He shuddered, sucked in a breath, and pulled away from the weapon.

"They didn't choose to die."

War shrugged. "Not my problem. I do what I was brought here to do."

"We're close!" Rachel yelled.

Becky tore her gaze away from War for a split second to see Rachel toss a poppy flower into the bowl.

War, taking advantage of the distraction, swung his sword sideways. She ducked and rolled away. The zing of the sword slicing through the air left goose bumps on her skin.

She jumped to a standing position again, planting her feet hip width apart. He charged forward. She used her sword to block. The clash of metal against metal lingered in the night air. Sweat dripped down her face.

The spot where he ran her through throbbed, but the skin was whole again.

"Let's see what this does."

An evil grin crossed his face and he turned away from her. He marched to the fire circle, stopping before his skin sizzled. With the wave of a hand, Leah flew through the air and over the side of the building.

"Leah!" Sarah yelled.

Sarah stood, staring at the place Leah went over, but Rachel pulled her back.

Becky ran forward, plunging the sword through War's back.

He staggered forward, caught in the flames, and pushed himself back, impaling himself deeper on her sword.

She yanked the weapon out of him. Anger and malice stared her down, but she wasn't afraid. This was what they'd been sent here to do. Angels were the warriors of God.

The rooftop door banged open. Her gaze flitted over to see Leah stumbling onto the roof. As she walked toward Sarah and Rachel, her injuries were healing.

"Can't get rid of me that easily," Leah said.

Relieved, Becky focused on War again.

In one spot in the circle, the flames were weaker. Barely flickering. War's eyes widened. "You won't be able to hold me here forever."

"Now!" Sarah yelled.

In unison, they recited the incantation to send him back. As she spoke the words, Becky continued to block sword blows and slice at War's sides. She moved in closer after one of the nicks to elbow him in the head. She jumped back.

As they recited the last line, she pulled a bottle of holy oil out of her pocket. With her teeth, she pulled the cork out. War advanced and she kicked out, glancing his shin. She poured the oil on her sword and swept the blade through the flames again. Then she plunged the weapon deep into his stomach until the tip came out his back.

He screamed.

She yanked the sword out of him. In a wisp of red smoke, he flashed out of existence.

The flames fueled by holy oil died.

Exhausted, they all crumpled to the ground.

***

In the loft minutes later, Becky sat in the armchair, using a little more angel power to heal her cuts. She ignored the bruises for now. Leah lay on the sofa, healing herself, losing some of the white in her wings. But they knew how to get it back. Later, they would figure out how to do the same for Rachel and Sarah.

Right now, all that mattered was they were all still in one piece. And War was gone. At least for now. She had no doubts the priest would summon him again, but it wouldn't be today. Or even next week if they were lucky.

For mortals, such a summoning ritual would drain them of energy for days at least.

"Hey, turn that up," Rachel said from the kitchen.

Rachel and Sarah, being the healthiest at the moment, sat in the kitchen at the breakfast island, facing the living room.

Becky leaned forward, groaning with the exertion, and picked up the remote. She hit the volume button three times.

"Word came into our station five minutes ago that the United States and Russia have agreed to talk in Ottawa. Other countries around the world have agreed to stop their fighting for now until peace talks are either successful or break down." Kevin Moore affected a sombre expression, but one that spoke of hope.

"That's good news," Sarah said.

Becky turned the volume down again.

"It is."

From the floor by the chair, a laptop pinged. Becky leaned over.

"I'll get it." Rachel rushed to her side, picked up the laptop bag, and put it in Becky's lap.

Becky smiled. "Thanks."

She withdrew the computer and opened the lid. The browser was still on the hacker forum. She had another red dot over the message icon.

LADYHACKER: MerlinCrackers agreed to a plea and to provide information. But they can't find Major-General Gunther Fertig anywhere to lay charges.

INVESTIGALHACK: How did you get that information so fast?

LADYHACKER: :) Talent. I've been checking every so often. It happened fast. I wanted you to know.

INVESTIGALHACK: Thanks. For everything.

Becky fished her phone out of her pocket and called her producer.

"Is it true?" She relayed what LADYHACKER had told her.

"Yes. All of it. To make sure countries keep the peace until the talks end, Canada is sending out peacekeepers. Because that's what we do."

"When are they doing that?"

"As soon as they all get their flu boosters. Plus, their other vaccines are up to date. They're getting fast-tracked for those."

She ended the call with her producer and filled in her sisters on what had transpired.

"With War gone, the peace talks should go well," Leah said.

"I hope so," Becky said.

They were in no shape to worry about any of the other horsemen yet, so Becky shoved thoughts of Conquest and Famine out of her mind. Once they were healed, feeling closer to one hundred percent, they would tackle Famine.

Rumblings of another gang war floated around the streets. Conquest's re-emergence had seen gang activity soaring. But the specialized divisions of the police department could deal with that.

"I think we need a little break," Becky said. "How about drinks at the bar? It's been ages since we've been there. Steve probably thinks we disappeared."

Sarah nodded. "And a late dinner."

Rachel hurried over to the sofa to help Leah up. "You think you can handle it?"

"For a burger and pop, you bet I can."

Becky pushed herself up from the chair. The pain that had been soaring was now a dull throb in places. And gone in others. In a day or two, she would be as good as new. Would any more tips come in while they were out? Just in case, she shoved her phone back into her pocket and grabbed her coat.

With War gone, a kernel of hope bloomed in her heart. The rest of the horsemen could wait. For now.

Thank you for reading Becky's story. I hope you liked spending time with her and her sisters.

Dear Reader,

Thank you for reading my book!

If you read Black Feathers, you know the original plan for the angels was to have one book with four angels all dealing with the four horsemen. Figuring out the points of view, and getting the whole story in the way I wanted to tell it, would have resulted in a huge tome. That's when I decided to give each angel her own book, dealing with her own horseman, and trying to figure out why she was exiled.

I really hope you loved the book as much as I did. Grey Feathers was fun to write and research, putting me in touch with some great people who answered a lot of questions for me. And of course credit goes to my husband for coming up with the titles of all the books. I was stumped with what to call them and I had to come up with something fast. The cover artist I wanted had an opening and she agreed to do the series, but she needed a title. Without missing a beat he rattled off all four titles.

There are four books in the series, but I suspect there will be more series in the angels' world. Stay tuned for that. You can sign up for my mailing list at https://cindycarroll.com/angelslist to be notified when new stories come out, plus get a copy of Fallen, the prequel short story.

Happy Reading,

Cindy

Acknowledgments

Writing a book is a solitary endeavour, but there are a lot of people who help along the way. I want to thank Hank Phillipi Ryan for answering my questions about being a reporter. I also reached out to a friend from years ago who is a reporter. The answers I received from Hank and my friend were invaluable with developing Becky's character. Any errors in the portrayal of a TV anchor and reporter are mine.

Thanks should also go to my writing group, Guelph Write Now, who keep me going when I just want to procrastinate. Those twice a month goals meetings help me stay on track.

About the Author

Cindy is a member of Sisters in Crime and a graduate of Hal Croasmun's screenwriting ProSeries. She writes screenplays, thrillers, horror, urban fantasy, science fiction and paranormals, occasionally exploring an erotic twist. A background in banking and IT doesn't allow much in the way of excitement so she turns to writing stories that are a little dark and usually have a dead body. She lives in Ontario, Canada with her husband and two cats. When she's not writing you can usually find her painting landscapes in oil, playing video games (Sims 3 and Sims 4 are favourites), or watching her favourite television shows marathon style.

Check out Cindy's website:
https://www.cindycarroll.com
Check out Cindy's other books:
https://books2read.com/cindycarroll

facebook.com/AuthorCindyCarroll

instagram.com/CindyPCarroll

goodreads.com/writesbooks

bookbub.com/authors/cindy-carroll